Unlawful Betrayal

UNLAWFUL BETRAYAL

a novel

Ruth Forrest Glenn

iUniverse, Inc.
New York Lincoln Shanghai

Unlawful Betrayal
a novel

iUniverse, Inc.

For information address:
iUniverse, Inc.
2021 Pine Lake Road, Suite 100
Lincoln, NE 68512
www.iuniverse.com

This novel is based on a true story.

ISBN: 0-595-27082-4

Printed in the United States of America

For daddy

Acknowledgments

I'd like to thank the many people who have encouraged me and upheld me through out the writing of this book. I thank my children for believing in me, but especially believing with me that all things are possible.

I'd also like to thank JJ for the hours she has spent reading for me and being a very good friend. She and my other friends and neighbors that have helped me keep going during the long days and nights of writing will always bring a smile to my face. Thank you Clip and Woody.

My gratitude and admiration to Sherry S. who took the time from her own schedule of writing and family herself, to know someone new and help pull them up with her. Her inspiration was a must in pulling this project together. You always love your first editor.:)

Thanks GC and Joni Stanley

I would like to take this opportunity to thank Benjamin M. Leroy for the time, wisdom, and kindness he has shown me in helping me pull together the books final most needed moments. I have learned more about procedures in publishing as well as how to successfully use my computer, because of him.

Last but not least, thank you dear readers for purchasing this book. May you also find your own visions, don't forget to dream big.

Prologue: Daddy's Girl

*R*enae was hardly noticed throughout school as she grew up. She was from a relatively poor family and lived on a farm outside of town. The school bus was her only escape from an abusive, alcoholic father, who fondled her sexually, since she was old enough to remember. He forced her to have intercourse with him, before she was eleven years old. She remembered the day his touching her vagina with his fingers was no longer adequate. He made her stroke his penis until he ejaculated then he would get up and leave her room. Renae was afraid to cry or make a sound during these episodes. Her father could become frightening in his anger if he couldn't get his own way. She had seen him beat her mother and brothers so severely, that they would stay in the house for weeks, unable to leave because of the black eyes, cracked ribs, and bruises. He would mostly masturbate over her unclothed body, and then pass out from the drinking. She was used to this by now. Renae's father seemed to be less likely to physically beat her than the others, as long as he was getting the sex he wanted from his daughter.

Several times she had tried to talk to her mother, but her plea was ignored. Her mother seemed unable to come to terms with such a thing.

Renae was worried that she might become pregnant by her father, but there was nothing she could do to stop him at this point.

There was a numbing effect inside of her, a new hardness, one that would form a terrifying dependence on and alliance to, the perverted abuse she had suffered. She couldn't help how she felt, she was in this enigma alone. Her emotions had shut down, as to out last the sentence she had been so unfairly condemned to endure.

It wasn't long, before Renae's father was coming to her often for intercourse. It was as though somehow she felt it her duty to satisfy his urges.

She dreamed daily of being set free from her captor. Reality however always was at the forefront of her mind, and the clouded nights of irreverent fetish would dispel with the light of day.

As Renae took her seat on the bus for another day of school, she thought how going to school was a relief for her. The awful incidents in her home took a pale back seat when she was into her school day.

She had daydreamed about the new boy at school, who had just moved to the area. He was in a few of her classes, and Renae couldn't help but notice him. She thought his sturdy black hair and physical stature made him a dream. In a moment of her rambling thoughts, the bus came to a halt.

The school bell rang, and the bus emptied quickly. Students were racing for the door as they always did. Renae wasn't ever in a hurry. She wanted to make the day last, as not to think of home.

As she started for the door in the crowd of students, she was bumped into and all her books knocked to the floor. Damn she thought! I can't be late for class. She stooped down to pick up her things, and as she did, the new boy's face met hers.

"Hi my name's Allen, what's yours?" he asked.

Stunned that he was talking to her, she answered softly, "I'm Renae."

He then helped her pick up all her books, and walked her to class. Renae was elated that he had noticed her. Allen seemed interested in her as well. He asked her if she would like him to give her a ride home after school.

Renae, timid on the inside but longing to exert herself, let out a "yes, oh yes! I'll meet you, over at the west side steps, about 3:00."

"I'll be there," said Allen.

A smile stayed on Renae's face the rest of the day. She couldn't keep focused, especially through her last class, then finally the bell rang, and class was out. She ran to her locker, and then out the doors on the west side of the building.

Allen was waiting there. She got into his car, feeling apprehensive as they headed for her home. They both laughed and smiled, enjoying each others conversation and company. Finally they were there. Renae had Allen stop just down the road, before dropping her off.

She got out of the car. "I'm sorry Allen, I can't invite you in." As she hung her head looking for the words to say, he reassured her that he understood, and he would see her tomorrow at school.

Renae had to keep Allen a secret. A cold sweat came over her. She knew this could mean extra punishment and abuse from her father if he were to find out. She began to cry. Her father was an angry man that beat his family, and was very possessive of her. When she told Allen these things, he said he didn't care about her father, and that he would sneak to see her. Allen wiped the tears from Renae's eyes, and told her he'd see her tomorrow.

They were soon dating on a regular basis. Renae would slither out of the house late at night, to be with Allen, as not to let her family know. It was hard to keep such a secret, but she was more afraid of never knowing any one who would love her because of her sordid life.

Their teenage love affair became ravenous. Renae was certainly not afraid of sexual intimacy, after all, sex was no stranger. She wanted to have a sexual relationship with Allen, and to stop the one she had been forced to have with her father for years now.

She would be eighteen in another week, and being her senior year, she was waiting with anxiety. Renae had explained to Allen that her father often abused her, and how she hated him, but was afraid to cause his anger to erupt. She didn't, however, tell Allen the entire truth, about the sexual relations she was having with her father. She was certain that Allen wouldn't want her, and it would ruin everything she needed. Even during the times she was making love with him, she was still having a sexual relationship with her father whenever she was home. With Allen she felt so cared for, but with her father, she felt so dirty and ashamed. She couldn't wait to be with Allen. He had asked her to move in with him as soon as she turned eighteen. He was a year older than her, and wanted out of his home as well.

The following week at school, a day before she was to turn eighteen, Renae felt nauseous. She threw up in the school restroom twice before the morning was over. She couldn't' seem to catch her breath. Her teacher sent her to the school nurse. Renae was so weak that she fainted.

The school nurse called an ambulance and they took her to the hospital. No one was prepared for the next announcement. The doctor who examined her told her she was pregnant, and approximately two months along.

Renae wasn't surprised, although she didn't want to think of the possibilities. This baby was in all probability her father's, but for her own sanity she would never utter a word of this. From that moment on she would only let herself think that the baby's father had to be Allen.

In fear she thought, how will I tell my parents and Allen? Then in the same breath, she said to herself, "My father won't tell anyone, or I'll tell everything." She would make her father feel her wrath, or at least a portion of it. Finally the hold on her would stop and now she suddenly felt a sense of power.

Allen rushed to see her at the hospital. He was concerned for her, and wanted to know what had happened. She began to tell him, but as soon as she mentioned the baby, he stopped her. He told her that he wanted her and his baby, and that they would find a way to make it work.

Renae and Allen quit school. Allen got a full time job in construction while Renae babysat a few children to make extra money. At first it seemed to be going well. Renae was finally out of her father's house and torment. Allen told her he wanted to be a good husband. Maybe she could relax in finally being loved by someone.

Their baby was born. They named him Jon. After the baby arrived, almost overnight things changed. Allen started to hang out with the guys from his job more than he was home. He was now drinking considerably.

Poor Renae, she had dreamed that Allen was the knight in shining armor that would fight all her dragons. But the more Allen drank, the more like her father he became.

Why had this happened? She was distressed with worry and despair. Only this time, she vowed it would be different. Allen was her husband not her father and she would assume the controls as his wife, with whatever opportunities presented themselves. She would force her marriage to work.

Renae learned to live with Allen and his lifestyle. With her heart crushed in an unhappy marriage, she poured all her efforts into loving and caring for this little child that had no say into the family in which he was born. Allen drinking heavily was no help or comfort really, so Renae just kept being the best wife and mother she knew how to be. Always being the caretaker since a little girl, she was used to the routine by this time.

The marriage survived while Renae harbored her discontent. She was pregnant each year, the children were no more than thirteen to fifteen months apart. By the birth of the fifth child, Renae knew she would never fulfill any dreams she had ever had. She should be content to have and love her babies. Often was the thought given that her oldest was really the son of her father, but she felt obligated to keep that secret to the grave for the sake of her son and her own.

Something abstruse was coming to collect from Rene, but she could not heed the augury nor change it's timing.

Allen had begun hitting her constantly, especially in places where others couldn't see the intrusive contusions. She could count on the surety that she would be abused by Allen sometime each day, unless he didn't come home. He was particular in his abuse of her breasts, and she suffered considerably for it. It was almost as though she had returned into the battering hands of her father. The only thoughts that were her own these days, were the dreams of a peaceful existence in a life she knew could never be.

Renae had recently walked in on Allen with their youngest child Jill. Allen had taken Jill's pants off of her. He was rubbing and caressing her between her legs, in an inappropriate way for a father. When Renae asked him what he was doing, he said there was nothing wrong with a daddy touching his daughter. Chills ran up and down her spine. She quickly made an excuse to Allen about doing something for the baby, and snatched Jill out of his hands.

For days Renae was distraught about the way she had seen Allen handle Jill. She knew that Jill was being singled out, just as she had been by her father for a sexual relationship. From that moment on, Renae would check Jill each day, to check for sexual scarring or penetration. I swear, she thought, I will do what ever I need to, to spare my daughter from the same fate as mine.

Renae gave her best effort to keep an eye out for Allen's abuse on the children. Though she tried to deflect any sexual perversion done against them, to her dismay, she was unable to control these events. There were indications that Allen was penetrating Jill's vagina with at the least his fingers. Renae knew it wouldn't be long before he was having intercourse with their daughter Jill. She was four when her father began trying to stretch her out so he could have his way with her.

There was a deep darkness that surrounded Renae, a repressed spirit that had been with her since she was a small child. It often scared her to think on it or to try to figure out what it was. When she felt great despair, this dark spirit over shadowed her thinking and seemed to know exactly where it was leading her whether she wanted to go along or not. She felt as though she was along for the ride, and not a unit of her own decisions. From the stories she had heard growing up about her family, it seemed that the generations had repeated many of the same patterns throughout the family lineage. Are we all doomed to repeat the folly of those who came before us, she wondered? Renae's depression had hardened and now more than ever she had lost all feeling. The numbness she had squelched had returned. How could she regain sanity or was there such a thing?

This dark feeling she had given into, led her to thoughts of Allen being gone. At first it was just him being gone from her life, but the more she fed on these thoughts, the more inviting it was that Allen just be gone from this world. Renae knew she would have to fight him to protect the children. She couldn't bear the concept of anything bad happening to them. The kids' love for her was the greatest gift she'd ever known. When thinking this, Renae would always push the thoughts of Allen dying away, and try to continue as usual.

What a saddened state of affairs their lives had become. Way out of control, so immensely surrounded by their own fears. The abuse was so bad, Renae would nervously shake. Sometimes she would sit on the floor and rock back and forth humming some tune from her childhood, usually after Allen beat her pretty badly.

Renae was rocking today. Allen hadn't been home for two days. That most likely meant a two day drunk for him, and a severe beating for her. As she rocked, Renae was reminded of the last time this had happened. The kids were always in bed early, especially if Renae saw something coming, and she always knew. She just wanted the children to be in bed asleep and pray that they wouldn't hear her screams.

Head-lights blared in the front window. It was late, and Renae was shaken into a decision. He couldn't beat me again, not now she thought, the slugs and kicks were taking their toll on her health. As weak as she felt, she just wanted to make it through this night alive and love her children one more day.

The door suddenly flung open. It was Allen. A bottle in one hand, and his keys in the other. They only exchanged glares. She never spoke first, that for sure got her a back of the hand across the head. They stared for what seemed like minutes. In a split second, the bottle in Allen's hand flew, hurling across the room. Before Renae could move out of the way, the bottle hit her head, laying her out flat on the floor.

Immediately she sat up, prepared for another blow. Once was never enough for Allen. If he hit her once, she would surely be hit again. Allen quickly lunged at her and wrestled her to the ground. He then sat on her stomach, and took her by the neck. With no mercy, he lifted her head off the floor from the base of her neck, and repeatedly banged her skull against the hard wood floor. While banging her head, he spit in her face and told her how worthless she was to him.

At one point during this struggle, Allen missed the floor and hit Renae's head against the iron leg of the wood burning stove. The next thing Renae saw, was Allen's fist coming towards her eye. She felt a surge of adrenaline and rose up off the floor in a rage.

"Don't hit me again Allen! If you hit me once more, I swear I'll kill you," Renae said as she ran back into the bedroom. This was unlike her quiet character. Something she had learned, was never to turn her back on Allen, or try to retaliate against him. She knew he would beat her worse for her rebellion.

This time, however, she was more afraid of not fighting back. Thinking her only chance of survival was a gun Allen kept in the corner by the bed. She lunged at the gun. Placing it into her hands, a rush of anger came over her. It was so fierce that it felt like all the anger she had ever known towards her father or Allen was screaming to exhale and be let out.

Allen laughed at her and arrogantly walked to the bedroom after her. He knew as countless times before that he could strike Renae and have his way with her. Something inside Renae snapped. Shaking, she faced him, finger on the trigger, ready to shoot.

Allen tried to patronize her. Keeping her down emotionally usually got him his own way. All Renae could think of was the sordid sexual events she had suffered all of her tragic life, the secret of her son, and that same sexual torment it seemed would now be repeated on her young daughter. It was so overwhelming to her that nothing Allen could say would slow down the pace of what was about to happen.

Allen charged toward her with a huge block of wood from the wood stove. Renae knew the very next thing she would feel was that wood against her head.

She let out an intense scream. "No more Allen. I can't take any more." She pulled the trigger. The piercing sound of the gun-shot made her ears ring. The shot blew right into Allen's chest. He fell to the floor writhing, and died in a deep scarlet pool of his own blood.

Renae, unable to think clearly, dropped to the bed, for what seemed to be hours, rocking back and forth as if that would erase what had just happened, or somehow soothe her pain. "What now? My children," she thought. What would happen to them all? She would surely have to go to prison for the crime of killing Allen. This family would forever be split up without a mother or a father now.

When the tears subsided, she could see Jill the youngest child standing in the doorway. Jill looked at her, then at Allen as he lay on the floor in his blood. What must she think? How would this affect a young child? Martyrdom forever?

Renae recalled the years of beatings and rapes she had received from Allen. They were over now. Allen couldn't abuse her any more, at least not physically. She didn't know if she would ever be free of the mental scourge.

Reality interrupted her torturous daydream. She was barely coherent of her surroundings, when she heard the sirens. It was as if rape had invaded her again. Renae, overcome by several policemen entering her home, was immediately arrested and handcuffed and taken away to jail.

The police stayed with the children until social services could get to the house, and take care of them.

Renae was tried and convicted of manslaughter. There was some favor found for her considering the tragic circumstances of her life. She was imprisoned, and her children became wards of the state, splitting them up into the foster care system. Except Jill, wouldn't speak to anyone. Social services felt it best to place her in an institution with special needs children.

Jill wouldn't remember for years what had happened that fateful night. She couldn't understand the dangerous irony. The experience of her father's crimson death and the sexual perversion he had done to her had scarred her character. Her future would reveal itself throughout her life, as if to signal the lusty mysteries ahead?

One year later, still living in the institution, Jill was adopted by an older couple who wanted children desperately. She would be their only child.

CHAPTER 1

I dreamed a handsome man would come into my life. He would sweep me off my feet and carry me into the sunset. Forever he would be mine, and we would be devoured in our own yearnings. Being consumed in a fire of passion that no label of society could affect. I could no more distinguish my lust from my cravings. I wanted this selfish kind of love, that would care only for me and what I needed.

I knew I could manipulate any situation to my advantage. Time was on my side, and I was patient. I was an only child and having my own way was simple. My parents were older when they had me, and it was easy to work them around to my way of thinking.

I indulged myself in books and movies. True love meant unsurpassed romance to me, that deeper relationship, a love so involved and intriguing that it was worth any risk too obtain. I never acknowledged any obstacles that would prevent me from achieving my goal. I felt the part of an amorous courtesan unraveling her fantasies.

That was one of the reasons I'd chose secretarial work as my college career. I enjoyed flirting, and mostly had an eye for the married man. I could play him so easily and there were never any commitments to worry about. At the first sign of him leaving his wife and getting too serious, I would bail out, making it sound as if he were too meritorious to leave his family. I insisted it must be me who left the relationship. This became a great way to have excitement in my life, but not to be tied down, or owe a man an explanation.

I'd been seeing married men since I was sixteen. No one really knew, because it was my secret. The first affair I had with a man fifteen years older than me. I was the regular babysitter for his children. It was the thrill of sneaking around and not getting caught that made it so alluring. Soon his wife found out, and put a stop to us seeing each other. For me it was an experience that fueled my appetite to continue seeing married men.

Time went by quickly after that last affair. My senior year was at its end. I had no steady boyfriend, but playing the field was interesting and tantalizing.

Tonight was my prom, what a wonderful evening it was. My date, had been a good friend to me since middle school. We had a good time together and were glad we could attend the prom just for the fun of it.

As I stood in the corridor waiting for my date to bring the car around, my mind was deep in thought of all I had learned over the years. This old high school wouldn't be a part of my life any longer.

I noticed a man walking toward me from the other end of the hallway. He made his presence known to me as I stood there alone. I knew he was married because he had been my science teacher the year before. Upon approaching me, he put his arm around me and spoke softly in my ear. "Do you need a ride home Jill?"

He caught me off guard. "No, thank you," I politely said. The moment seemed to last a long while. Then abruptly my date entered the hallway and without hesitation I said, "Goodnight Mr. C. It was a good year, wasn't it." I liked teasing and being the one in control.

I was finally finished with high school, and looking forward to summer vacation. It was good to be eighteen and feel some authority with freedom from school and parents. This summer was going to be great. I was getting ready for some wild fun. A bunch of my girlfriends and I were going to hang out at the beach. We wanted to flirt with the men that came our way. Everything was so carefree, almost boring for me after a while. There wasn't any excitement in hanging around with men my own age.

I soon found myself alone, reading romance novels, or daydreaming about that special guy. Either way I was bored. There had to be a way to spice up my summer and my life. Things were too dull, and I wasn't about to let any opportunity for a thrill to pass me by.

I decided to fill the car with gas in the morning, and head for the city. I only lived an hour away from Chicago, and thought it'd be fun to meet some friends, go shopping and out to dinner.

Maybe tomorrow, I'd see him somewhere and ultimately meet the man in my passions and dreams. If I did, I wasn't letting go. Ever.

CHAPTER 2

*I*t was 6:00 a.m. when the alarm sounded. I hadn't slept well, tossing all night in bed with anticipation of my city trip. Good thing it was a Saturday. There was less work to do on Saturdays, and it was great being able to feel more relaxed about my day's events.

You could smell breakfast cooking. I have to eat when I first get up. This was probably because my mom always spoiled me, and cooked all my meals. I was soon dressed and ready to leave. I wanted everything to be perfect today, my nails, hair, clothes, everything. If I met him, I'd be ready for the experience. Finally I was in my car. I started the engine and waved goodbye to mother. She was doing the morning dishes, and I could see her in the kitchen window as I pulled the car out of the driveway.

This feels great, I thought. What a beautiful day! A look at the fuel gage told me I needed to stop for gas. Damn! I'd just passed the station I always used. I had to think for a moment if another gas station was on my way. Ah! The "Red Tank" gas station on the edge of town. Just my luck, the station was packed.

Finally my turn came. I was glad this station was full service. I hated pumping my own gas. It always left my hands dirty, and I just didn't like the menial task of doing it myself.

Then I saw him. WOW! He was excessively admirable. I had to stare. He was very tall and dark featured, with black hair swept over in a wave. His eyes were a serious blue. They seemed penetrating, as though he was able to look right through a person. His skin looked smooth and tanned with an olive glow to his complexion. He was filling up another car when I saw him.

The attendant asked me, "Fill it up ma'am?" Oh excuse me, yes, I would like the tank to be filled, thank you. As the attendant was filling the tank, I decided I'd go inside and pay for the gas. The attendant was pleasant and said, "Alright just give your money to Daniel, he's right in there." I turned to look, and it was him. His name was Daniel. I had to meet this guy. I would gladly wait my turn in line, to get to him.

It didn't take long to get to the counter to pay for my gas. "That'll be fifteen dollars," Daniel said, "And please come again."

"Oh I will, I will," I looked up just in time to see him wink at me.

Getting back into my car, I remembered I was in a hurry to get moving, or I would be late to meet my friends in Chicago. The entire day, through shopping and restaurants, I couldn't keep my mind from thinking about my encounter with Daniel. There wasn't anything that sounded more exciting, or that could take my thoughts off wanting to know this guy.

Finally the day was over, and it was time for the trip back home. I welcomed it, now I could be alone with my fantasy about Daniel and myself. I loved mystery, and the dark side of romance. Who was he? Was he married? Did he have children? Even if he was married, would that stop him from having an affair or following his own desires? I had to pursue knowing him just in case there was a chance.

Daniel was obviously older than me, but that was also a trait I was looking for in a man, older, established, able to take care of me.

The hour ride home seemed to fly by, finally I pulled into the driveway. I was exhausted and glad to be home. I got ready for bed thinking seriously about Daniel, and wondering how I was going to get him to be interested in me. Before realizing it, I had dozed off.

Morning came fast. I needed to visit a few friends today. The town I lived in was small, and most people knew someone else's business. This wasn't an unusual description for a small mid-west town. I knew I could be clever and discreet on a Sunday, and investigate this man, Daniel.

Through my inquisitive nature, I found out Daniel was thirty-eight years old, making him twenty years my senior. He was also married some fifteen years and had a son and three daughters, ranging in ages seventeen and under. Daniel's wife Emily was overweight and insecure, not living in the real world mentally or tending to her family's needs properly. Emily seemed to be consumed with her man, and the control of her family. I was told she was mentally ill.

I started buying all of my gas, at the Red Tank station. I began hanging out there, or anywhere else Dan was, just so he'd notice me. After weeks of forcing myself in his direction, finally in a local restaurant, Dan saw me and sat down at my table.

The Windrow was a quiet restaurant. It had its family room with dining tables, covered with blue table clothes. In another section, was a bar that offered liquor drinks, as well as pie and coffee. I have always liked the booths near the bar. They were so private and intimate, with white table clothes and fresh cut flowers. The leather on the seats are soft and posh. I felt so feminine and tranquil there.

Where I had been so bold before, I was now feeling quite shy. Daniel began the conversation, and soon we were laughing and talking together. He never mentioned his wife or kids once. He told me I was beautiful, and that he had been aware of my presence at a lot of similar places he went, too. We held each other in a gaze with our eyes that I had never experienced before with anyone.

Everything in me surged to a heightened level. In a fleeting moment, I reached for his hand, and touched him. I had knocked over the fresh flowers and spilled them on the table. I felt so embarrassed. Flushed, I looked up to see Dan's face. He wasn't across the table any longer and his lips quickly met mine. We held our lips in a kiss that was the most intense osculation I had ever encountered. He pulled away slowly, and excused himself saying he had to leave.

"Will I see you again?" I asked. I couldn't take my eyes off of his physique, as he walked toward the doors of the restaurant.

He turned and smiled saying, "You most certainly will, Jill."

Between my hanging around at the gas station that Daniel managed, and our meetings at restaurants, we spent as much time together as we could. The Windrow would remain our favorite spot, and that first meeting would always linger in my mind. I fell deeply in love with Dan, and to my amazement he fell for me. He was very handsome. It took my entire strength just to hold back forcing myself on him sexually. Soon casual encounters weren't enough. I had to find a way to see more of him, and in a much more intimate setting. I thought of a plan that would make more time for Dan and I. I applied as a nurse's aide in the same nursing home as Daniel's wife, Emily. If I could befriend her, then she would let me come to her home. Emily would never be the wiser and I could see Dan anytime I wished.

This plan worked. I bought Emily presents, pretending to be her friend. The sad thing was, I started to enjoy my time with her. This went on for quite a while. Things were working fine this way. We were even able to have sex in Daniel and Emily's bed when Emily and the kids were gone from home. Dan and I had been meeting in a secluded local cemetery, to make love in his car. We spent time with each other wherever we could, and sexual pleasure was the biggest thrill of our relationship. My desire for him only grew, along with my obsession to make him mine. I couldn't get him out of my head.

We were parked in his car, and had been together all evening. Daniel was rubbing and caressing my body. We undressed and clinched each others bodies ardently. My hand, rubbing his penis while his lips kissed mine. It was only a fleeting moment it seemed, before we were both deep into sexual bliss and to stop at that point would have been fallacious. I could forget it all when Daniel was inside of me. Our hearts pounded together as he thrust himself in and out of my body during our love-making. His hands completely holding and caressing me. I was having palpitating feelings in places I didn't know existed in my body's sensuality. Each movement was a stroke against another source of pleasure. Obviously I'd never been with a real man. Dan was not like anyone else. He was ready, and reached climax with not much intervention from me. We would just hold each other and breathe until our hearts simultaneously beat as one. It couldn't be any better than this. Wherever we did it, it was the best. I was completely hooked like a drug addict waiting for the next fix.

CHAPTER 3

*B*eing around Dan's children was interesting. I felt empowered to manipulate them all, except for his daughter, Kathy. As far as Emily was concerned, I'd become part of the family. She didn't have a clue about her husband's and my relationship.

Daniel had been a deputy sheriff before managing the Red Tank station. He accidentally found out the sheriff was embezzling county funds. When he went to speak to Sheriff Ross about this, Ross fired him. Dan then decided he would retaliate by running for sheriff. The Royce family and I campaigned to help Daniel win the election.

We portrayed him as a family man, true blue to the end. The kids and their smiling faces helped Dan gain favor at the polls. Time went by fast and the election was here. The night of the primary election, we all sat around the Royce kitchen table. A lot of Dan's neighbors and friends were there to wait for the election returns. To everyone's disappointment he lost the primary by eighty-one votes in the entire county. We were so discouraged, but the polls were closed and he had lost.

Within a few weeks many of the town's people were encouraging Dan to run for sheriff in the general election. The catch here would be he would have to run as an independent party candidate instead of splitting the Republican ticket. So for the next few months, we were campaigning again with the hopes that the eighty-one votes we'd missed before, would come over to Dan's side.

November came, and the election was on. Again we found ourselves around the Royce kitchen table, waiting for election returns. Over the evening, Dan picked up more and more votes. Finally the count was in. We were all impatient to hear the outcome. The radio announcer broke for a brief message, when he returned he stated, we now have all the ballets in for the office of county sheriff. The room was silent, not even a sigh.

The announcer began, "It seems that Daniel Royce has won the office of Onion County Sheriff." Yells and screams went up by all. Everyone was congratulating him. I knew I had to wait until we were alone at one of our secret places to really show my appreciation for him.

Before Dan would take office in January, he needed to think of the people he wanted to work with. He needed a secretary, and a deputy. There was a lot he had to consider. He also saw a need to assess what the sheriff's office lacked. He went to work right away and met with the board of supervisors. He convinced them he needed two deputies instead of one, and regular patrol cars instead of the sheriff's private vehicles. Dan had his work cut out for him, but we were on our way. I felt so intoxicated with the man he was, and with his sudden authority as an elected official.

I desired to be his secretary. Daniel knew this and wanted me to work for him as well. Emily was insanely jealous of any woman near her husband. I began to complain to her about being a nurse's aide. I didn't like the job and wanted to have a career where I could use my clerical skills. I was trainable and willing to learn. Emily ate it up. She was convinced she'd rather have me in that office than another woman she didn't know. Soon she was overstating my case to Dan.

Before long and with little planned resistance from Daniel, I was hired. This was going to be great! We could see each other every day and meet whenever we wished. It was a license to steal. What could be more perfect for our affair?

Dan and I were set, and wore the office proudly. He gained his two deputies, new squad cars, and immediately moved his family into the sheriff's house, across the street from the court house downtown. The sheriff's house had the jail built off the back porch. The house itself was built in the 1800s. Next was how to keep Emily busier than she already was, so we could continue our affair. We came up with the perfect solution. She would make a great matron of this jail, cooking, cleaning, and doing laundry for the prisoners. This was a better plan than we could ever have imagined. Between her work outside the home, children, and being matron of the jail, Emily would never know what hit her. I liked the plan.

CHAPTER 4

Working with Dan was a dream come true for me. When we were the only ones in the office, we'd talk and discuss our future plans together. Daniel and I decided to open a bank account and save for the day we would be married. Daniel always cashed his checks first, and then brought the cash to Emily, so she could budget the home expenses. This made it easy for him and I to save money, because Emily never really knew, what his checks amounted to.

Daniel earned over thirty-thousand per year. At that time in 1972, that was a decent wage plus benefits. However, Daniel was able to take a few thousand a year off the top, and say he made less. The extra money he added to our account gave us quite alot to work with.

He never did save any money for his children, or anyone but us. The bank account was in my name for private purposes. Daniel trusted me.

He helped me put a down payment on a home. I had to move out of my parent's house, before they suspected our affair. The house we bought was Emily's uncle's old home. Emily often told me the story of her uncle, and how his wife kept having affairs. One day the uncle came home, and was so distraught about his marriage, that he used his oven and gassed himself to death. I didn't care about the story. The house needed to be remodeled and we had the money, so Dan and I began to build a future with this home. It looked like a doll-house when we were finished with the work on it. All my fantasies were becoming reality.

Daniel's job required a lot of work away from home. So we would meet often. Eventually someone told Emily about us. We had to reassure Emily that our relationship was purely a working one. Emily was extremely gullible and only needed to be consoled.

I was at their house constantly. Sometimes the screen would be locked. I would snip the wire on the back screen door, and unhook the door and go on in. As far as I was concerned, Dan wanted me there and I was welcomed anytime whether the rest of his family approved or not. I was extremely jealous of one person though, Dan's younger teenage daughter, Kathy. Kathy was pretty, with blonde hair down to her waist. She was tall and slender with green eyes. Kathy wasn't very close to her mother, but she seemed to be a daddy's girl. I wanted the place she had in her father's eyes. I wanted it all.

I quickly picked up on the turmoil between Kathy and her mother. I had a marvelous, yet horrid thought. I would cause constant friction by interfering in the children and Emily's relationships. The family would be so busy fighting with each other they'd have no idea about Daniel and my plans.

I was successful. The family was soon a house literally divided. Daniel hated his home, he fought constantly with his wife. I would always be waiting for him to run to me. I loved the need he had for me. Daniel and I had Emily convinced that she shouldn't talk to her children or press them for answers about their day or anything else. I know Emily was frustrated and angry, begging Dan for his love and sex. I made Dan promise me he wouldn't have sexual relations with Emily again. I'm fairly certain he didn't, and that was one of the reasons Emily seemed so sad and unsure of her marriage.

Several times I asked Daniel to leave her, but he would say he couldn't because of his public job and his children. But I knew deep down he was selfish in his desires just like me, and the real reason he wouldn't leave was his pride. The sheriff's family carried a lot of why he was elected. An honest family man was how the election had portrayed him.

Preston, which was the county seat, was extremely rough for a small town. Drugs were rampant, and it was becoming a very dangerous place. I became deputized just so I could legally ride along as an extra deputy and spend time with Dan, transporting prisoners.

One evening, a man's head was split open with a steel bar during a brawl. The police and sheriff's departments were called in. It was two troublesome families who were always in conflict with the law. The law officers used tear gas to quiet the crowd on Union Street. Several people were arrested and placed in jail.

The jail being in the back of the sheriff's house meant dragging prisoners through the Royce home, either through the back porch, or the living room entry. There were ten prisoners locked up that night.

This meant ten meals a day for Emily to prepare, besides meals for her own family. That ought to keep her busy and off Dan's back, I thought. Never once did I care what I was doing to five other people's lives. I just couldn't care. If I did, It'd be over and I'd have to give this easy, lusty affair up.

We had Emily so frantic. She didn't know what was going on. One evening as visiting hours were just ending for the jail, Emily and I went to lock the back porch doors, and in through one of the doors busted a very hard and rough looking young woman. This woman argued to see her brother in jail.

Emily explained visiting hours were over and the woman would have to leave. All of a sudden the woman threw her fists and slugged Emily in the face. Before I realized what was happening, we were all throwing fists and in a physical struggle with this girl. Daniel's daughter Kathy saw this from the kitchen and called the police who came within minutes, and arrested the woman who had attacked us.

Not long after the incident, Daniel met up with the woman's husband and brother, and there was another man with them. He had stopped them on a routine traffic violation that had turned dangerous. Daniel at that time still only carried one bullet in the chamber of his gun, and a nightstick for protection. These men saw Dan was alone and took advantage of the opportunity. The three men knocked Dan down to the ground, and beat him, with his own nightstick. As they struggled with him, Dan was able to shoot the one bullet off as a warning and get rid of it, so they couldn't kill him with it. The men kicked his jaw and head repeatedly, busting his facial bones severely, and breaking his dentures.

It was the fourth of July weekend, and getting Dan into a hospital for surgery was very hard. He would have to wait the weekend. It was extremely painful for him, and his face swelled three or four times larger than normal. Emily, Dan and I all went to Chicago, to admit him into the hospital.

As they wheeled Dan away to the emergency room, I took Emily's arm and persuaded her to go sit down in the waiting room. As we sat there I began to talk to Emily, and mold her around to my way of thinking. I convinced her that she shouldn't pressure Daniel about anything now, especially sexual intercourse for quite some time. I told her Dan was so worn out, and needed to recover from his wounds. Emily reluctantly agreed.

Daniel also openly blamed Emily for his jaws being broken. He accused Emily of provoking the girl that evening on the back porch. Although this was probable, it wasn't all her fault. It did make more of a gap between Daniel and Emily, making Emily more insecure than she already was, and she, too, blamed herself.

CHAPTER 5

*I*t was hard for me to get used to not seeing Dan as much while he was home ill and recovering from his broken jaw. I tried to go visit him when Emily had to work. Then I could have time to caress him and do sexual favors for him orally and in other ways that appealed to us. We did manage to keep our back street romance alive. After six months Daniel was able to eat solid food again. He and his wife had grown farther apart, and we'd been seeing each other for quite sometime now.

Emily was a nervous wreck. She knew something was wrong in her marriage, but in her ignorance, she still trusted me, and believed everything I was telling her. She soon was seeing doctors regularly, thinking she was having a nervous breakdown. Finally she found a doctor who prescribed her tranquilizers. She was to take them two times a day.

Emily was always grouchy and disorientated from taking her medication. It was so easy to use her, and take advantage. Sometimes she would invite me over for tea. I would take the opportunity to put an extra pill of her medication in her cup. Drugged out she was more easily controlled. Destruction was coming for Emily, and there was no escape.

Meanwhile Dan's oldest daughter, Ann, left home for college. Ann was ready to leave all the fighting and screaming that her mother seemed to thrive on. Leaving such turmoil was something to look forward to, indeed. Ann was so disgusted and embarrassed by Emily, she couldn't wait to get away from home. I was glad that there would be one less Royce child to deal with.

With Ann gone, that left Kathy, Sherri, and Brian. All of whom were very unassuming where I was concerned. Kathy was my target. She was distraught most of the time. Emily left all responsibility of the two younger kids up to her, and she beat and traumatized her to extremes. Kathy was so afraid of Emily, and had too much accountability for a child her age. Dan had said that throughout the early years of their marriage, Emily had been mean and controlling. She had always physically and emotionally battered Kathy, throughout Kathy's childhood, and even into her teen years. On the other hand, I could use this pattern of abuse as my way into a closer friendship with Kathy, giving Dan and I more control.

Emily began to walk for hours at night, when Dan was out working with me. She walked for miles, and was often dazed and confused. She couldn't get herself together, and I was glad of her problems. After all she didn't love Daniel like I did. She deserved to lose him in her stupidity. Daniel, as smart as he was, was still easy prey for me. I had become diligent in my excursion to make him solely mine.

Daniel started to aggressively participate in playing this destructive game with me. He would do whatever I asked. We had to prove to the community that Dan served, that Emily was unstable. If we could prove this, we would be on our way in succeeding to keep Dan's job, and the ultimate goal of putting Emily in a mental institution. This would of course lead to their divorcing and Daniel could marry me.

Through our conversations we tried to convince Emily that she really needed a close, caring friend. I told her I was that friend, and that I would help her. She was heavily burdened with the fact that she and Dan were not getting along and that he had stopped having sex with her for quite some time. As Emily continued to tell me these private things, I couldn't help but gloat over the entire situation. Everything she spoke of would answer my questions or give me more incentive for my cause. How could she be so foolish and ready to trust? I think she was desperate for the control of her life and marriage, she used to think she had. Now however, she had no control over her children or her husband. If not me, some other woman could have taken Emily for all she had. It might as well be me.

I saw nothing as an obstacle in reaching my destiny. Emily needed much emotional reassuring. I soon pressured her into going to a mental health service. She was quick to latch onto things, but not to let go. Once she got the idea she should go to therapy, Dan let her know in anger, that neither he, nor his children would be going with her. Again she stood alone. With no family support, she was entirely wrapped up in her own insecurities and made the decision not to go to therapy.

Kathy was worn out at her young age. Emily had worked her to physical extremes in the name of housework. Inside, Kathy was building a fierce rebellion. Work was all she knew. She was never allowed time to be happy about being a teenager. Emily brought such a morbid atmosphere into their home. She would kick Kathy back under the bathroom sink and toilet areas if Kathy hadn't cleaned things to her satisfaction. It could be something as minor as a small hair left on the bottom of the toilet. Emily kicked Kathy so often, that she hated taking showers after gym class at school. Because of the black and blue marks on her body, she skipped out quickly after gym, and being her last class, she'd just go home. She saw to the needs of her younger siblings, plus was in charge of cleaning the large house her family lived in. Kathy did all of the dishes and, laundry, and cooking for the prisoners also, besides her family's household chores. Emily spared no mercy.

Although Daniel and I knew we had set the home up to be a drastic environment, especially because of Emily's mental illness, we chose to look the other way. I felt no sense of conscious about the trauma that was being inflicted upon Dan's children. I mean, my mother wasn't always good to me either, so I chose to dismiss the Royce children's dilemma.

One evening, Dan returned home earlier than expected. To his surprise he found Kathy sitting at the top of the stairway with her hands on the sides of her head and her face between her knees. Over Kathy stood Emily, who weighed over three hundred pounds, to Kathy's one hundred. Emily with closed fists was repeatedly punching Kathy on her back and neck.

Kathy at sixteen, and thin, was no match physically to conquer Emily's anger. Daniel, seeing this, did something out of the ordinary. He ran up the stairs, grabbed Kathy and moved her out of the way, and pushed Emily down the stairs.

Emily fought forcefully. She tore Dan's shirt, and slapped his face, even ripping his clothing right off his back. She seemed almost possessed with such evil and rage.

After that incident, the physical beatings would still continue to dominate the children's lives, until each child left home to get away from her.

When Kathy, on her eighteenth birthday, was punched with Emily's fist, she was knocked up against a second story window. The glass broke and she started to fall outside. Her brother, Brian, grabbed her arm and pulled her back in the house. It did no good for Dan's children to run away from Emily. If she was going to beat them, she chased them everywhere, across beds, furniture etc., grabbing ankles, wrists, whatever she could until she caught them. She was a monster, and Dan and I had helped create her.

That evening of Kathy's eighteenth birthday after that immense physical battle, she packed her few belongings and moved down the street into a sleeping room.

Now I could make a direct move for Kathy. In her desperation I would take her into my home, and appeal to her need for someone, at least for a while.

CHAPTER 6

The Royce home now had only the two younger children living in it. After Kathy left, Emily proceeded to continue her physical abuse, and directed it mostly on Sherri and Brian. By this time though, the younger kids were so numb to her blows that they fought back. When Emily realized they wouldn't take her beatings, and they hit her, there were fewer physical attacks by her on them. I took my attentions and focused them on Kathy and Dan. There was more work to be done in sealing my fate with Daniel. We were always together and having sexual relations beyond expectation. I didn't want it to stop.

I approached Kathy with the idea of moving into my home. This way I could actively steer her in whichever direction I desired. I created a depressing atmosphere for her. I set up house rules such as, whenever she came home, if the screen door was locked she must go away for a couple of hours, because this meant her father and I were having sex and couldn't be disturbed. Kathy really had no one and seemed lonely. She knew not to cross me, and for a while she didn't.

Not more than a month went by before I'd convinced Dan that Kathy was a poor judge of character, and was running with the wrong crowd of friends. I told Kathy she had to move and find somewhere else to live, that she was an embarrassment to her father, and his office of sheriff. This left her homeless, and soon she was begging her abusive mother to let her move back home. Emily, in her own selfishness, refused Kathy's request. Emily continued to follow Kathy to the bars and public places, leaving notes on her car, condemning her for living on the streets. She kept taking unusually long walks at night. The walks were noticed by the people in the community. Police officers would stop her as a figure in the dark, then they'd find out who the night shadow was, and they'd send Emily on her way.

The law enforcement of Preston thought it was fun to ridicule and rip apart a family. It was quite the talk of the town. Her walks were a way for her to look for Daniel and me. She would walk for hours in all kinds of weather to find Dan. She even lost continence sometimes, and wet herself before she would get home. Kathy always took care of Emily, when she lived at home, getting clean clothes for her and such. Daniel thought it was amusing that Kathy often had to put Emily to bed in her disorientated state. Emily was a very sick person yet still mean and stubborn, so you couldn't feel too sorry for her.

Sometimes I had to take my mind off of Emily Royce, or I'd go crazy. There was plenty of gossip in the law center to keep me busy. Half the staff was having an affair with someone else's wife or husband. There was Renee the county treasurer, and Bill the district court judge. Even Henry Dorth who sang and led his church choir, was sneaking around with the church organist.

I think most particular in our little circle was Malaine Rabinski and Bob Wolfe, the county attorney and his secretary. Now there's a steamy romance. That's why our little internal affairs group was so shocked when we heard Bob was cutting off the affair and staying with his wife.

Malaine was very unhappy and threatened to tell Bob's wife everything. Then things seemed to calm down for a couple of days. On Friday the friction started again. Malaine had been drinking that evening, and drunk as she was, she called Dan's house to talk to Emily. According to Emily, Malaine said she'd like to borrow Daniel, since Emily lent him out as a stud.

Emily was furious. She slammed the phone down, and ran across the street to the court-house to tell Daniel what had just happened. Dan and I were in the office, so I couldn't help but over hear everything Emily said and Dan's reaction to it. He was angry and told Emily to get her ass home, and never speak of this incident again, to anyone.

The more Dan and I discussed what Malaine had done, the angrier we became. How dare she open her mouth? She could expose everyone's affairs. She had her time in the sun. She shouldn't be such a bitch, and let others have their time. We decided to give Malaine a visit and tell her off.

However, we couldn't take a chance of being seen at her house. In exhausting all avenues, we knew just a quiet walk up the alley would be the only path to go to her home.

The strangest thing took place as we approached Malaine's house. Dan and I both noticed a large figure of a person in the dark, leaving out the back door. We couldn't make the figure out, whether it was man or woman, and we didn't feel we should acknowledge the person, so we watched and waited until the figure left in silence.

A few minutes passed and we decided to knock on the door to speak with Malaine. Slowly, Malaine answered the door. She was quite drunk and antagonistic. She invited us in. Once inside, Malaine kept her focus on Daniel and made several flirting comments toward him. When he told her never to call his house again and make the remarks she had made to Emily, she became flippant. She then made the comment that she'd really like to have a night in bed with Dan, and show him what a real woman felt like.

I reared at her and pushed her down to the floor calling her a slut, and telling her she would never be with Daniel. Malaine looked up from the floor, and just stared at Dan and me. She bowed her head and sat there. We were both angry at her, dragging us into her problem. We decided it would be best if we left.

Walking out of the house into the dark night, we headed up the alley and back to the sheriff's office. As we walked away, on impulse, I turned around and looked at Malaine's house one more time. When I did, I saw entering her house, the same large figure we had seen before, as we were coming up the walk to her door. Dan and I just walked faster to get away. After some paper work at the sheriff's office, we decided to call it a night and go home. It was about 3:00 a.m.

Later on that morning when the office opened for the day, I noticed it was full of people. The chief of police, county attorney, and the state's attorney were all there. One of our deputies came out of the office.

"What's going on, Tom?" I inquired.

He proceeded to tell me that last night for some mysterious reason no one is sure of, Malaine Ranbinski was found dead behind a chair in her home. The assumption from the investigation was she had been so intoxicated that by falling, or by a push of some kind, she was unable to get up and breathe. Suffocation is listed as the cause of death. It was the strangest thing, the doctor found unexplained bruises and scratch marks on her throat.

Soon there was a sort of list of potential enemies of Malaine's, possibly someone who would benefit if her mouth were shut for good. The county attorney, of course, was the first on the list because of their affair. Malaine had made him the executor of her will, just a few weeks before she died. Next there was Emily Royce who was already unstable, and had reason to not like Malaine. Then it was Daniel Royce, and myself, Jill Sterns, last was the police chief, Allen Wrestler, whom had his own affairs to cover up. Everyone was so hushed about talking this situation over.

Malaine's family was extremely anxious about knowing what had exactly happened to her. The county attorney had the power to order or deny an autopsy. Since Bob Wolfe had much to hide, he just wanted Malaine buried and forgotten about. Therefore, his judgment was against an autopsy and there was nothing else left to do but bury her and move on.

We all had a secret to tell, and this callow woman stood in the way for many of us at this point. I was relieved after the funeral was over. There never was any further investigation on the case.

Years later though, it was made known to Dan, that a former deputy of his had the original list of murder suspects, and that Emily, Daniel and I were still major suspects on it. This man also possessed photographs of the victim. Daniel and I were apprehensive of her death. When I pushed her, could that have been the final demise? We thought we left her very much alive. Why were we serious suspects? No one could place us at her home, the night she died, we were so careful to walk down the alley in the dark to get there.

Where did Emily fit into this mess? The most chilling thought to me was who was the dark figure that left as we approached Malaine's house, and entered it as we left.

After a few months, the accusations and inquiries about her death slowly disappeared. Dan and I were always careful about our affair after this, because we never wanted this case to resurface. Being tried for a murder was a fight we didn't want to face. We erased all files in the computer on Malaine, and were sure to cover our tracks.

Now, I even had Dan where he had to always remain in a relationship with me. I pushed Malaine down on the floor that night, and maybe she couldn't get back up, thus she suffocated. If that was how she died, Daniel saw it all, and never spoke of it, or admitted we were there. That would make him an accessory to murder, and if I went down, he would go down, and he knew it. This gave us one more sick little secret, that bonded us closer together.

CHAPTER 7

I was glad when things at the law center got back to normal. Daniel still wanted to wait to leave his marriage until all his children were grown. It sounded good, but he was selfish just like me, and he just had cold feet. As long as he was sheriff, he didn't want a divorce. He didn't think it looked good to the public as an elected official. So he strung Emily along, had a relationship with me and continued as sheriff.

I was practically living at his and Emily's home. I would entice Dan by buying new clothing and pretending to try them on for Emily. I was really showing off my figure in front of Daniel so he'd want me even more. Emily got so tired of me being there. She would fight with Dan in front of me, trying to ignore me. There was nothing she could do about it, because he would argue with her and say that I was just like one of the kids, and I could come over whenever I liked.

Kathy and Ann told Emily that Dan and I were having an affair, but she refused to acknowledge this information. She was so blind and lacking in wisdom of any kind. She became more physically violent to Dan and her children all the time. It wasn't apparent how she was driven, but something ghastly possessed her.

I, on the other hand was happy with Dan and our relationship. Emily was out there mentally and her unforgiving puritanical thoughts were choking her to death. She loved the underdog label, and she played the victim in her life so long, that she was the casualty of her own war.

My mother and father were getting older now. I was trying to visit them more often. They knew about Dan and me now, but tended to turn their heads the other way.

Out of the blue one day, my mother called me and said that my father had had a heart attack and died suddenly.

I hurried home. She was sad and needed my comfort. I was shocked, my daddy couldn't have died. I kept seeing the face of this other man. The more I concentrated on my father, I couldn't place who the man was. The more I thought on this the more I saw his face. I felt the mysterious man I kept seeing was also someone who had hurt me once in an unusual way. What was it? Oh well, I couldn't dwell on anything else right now. The sordid visions would have to wait until I had more time to think. Later she would tell me something that would change my life forever. We set up the funeral and buried dad, spending a lot of time together those few days.

During one of our conversations, she explained how she and dad couldn't have children, so they decided to adopt. Babies were so hard to adopt, because there weren't many, and everyone wanted them. However they wanted a child so badly, that they looked even at handicapped children. In their quest they found me. I was four years old and living in the state facility for retarded and handicapped children. The nurses told them they thought I was deaf, because I never spoke, but used sign language. Then they found I was able to speak, it was just that I'd been placed with the deaf children and mimicked them and my surroundings. They believed I'd be fine with a good home and love.

So Thelma and Fred Sterns adopted me, and I became Jill Sterns. I was shocked. I was so close to my father, or so I thought. He never told me. Why? It was like we had never talked even though we'd spent a life-time together. At first I was angry, but it was so long ago, and I just needed to get over the loss of the only father I'd ever known. The time lapse, dulled the effect of this information.

My mother reluctantly gave me the name of my birth mom, and as much knowledge as she knew. I began to search for my biological mother. I soon found out, information, I wished I'd never known. My birth mother was a convicted felon, and had been imprisoned for the last twenty years, and was still there. I couldn't recall her at all, but something kept gnawing at me about her.

I also found I had brothers that had been given away, there was no way to know what all their names were at this point, but I did find information about two of them. It was scary. I discovered they both had extensive criminal records.

Dan and I used every resource available to find out who my family was, but every search led to a dead end of crime, and questionable character with the law. Finally I'd seen enough. I figured I would cut my losses, and be glad I had been adopted.

After a year or more of searching, I gave up, and never brought the subject up again. All of this information about where I'd came from, made Daniel and I much closer. He felt sorry for me and I was loving the attention. With my father gone, and what I knew about my biological family, I could go on again with some finality to my life. As far as I was concerned, Mr. and Mrs. Sterns were, and always had been, my parents.

CHAPTER 8

Dan's and my sex life was just starting to reach its peak. We never seemed to make love enough. Every time we were alone together, in any situation, my breathing would become erratic. I was willing to try anything with Daniel. He was a good lover to me. His hands were always smooth, and glided along my body's curves, ravishing my pulse points. We had intercourse in so many unusual places, even in the sheriff's office after hours. The desk became an inside joke to us, I've laid on it so often. We would touch each other throughout the day, building to a climax by the time the day was over. It was so thrilling. We could have been caught having sex at any time. Daniel truly loved my ample breasts, and I made sure they were always displayed well, in whatever I was wearing.

Sometimes a salesman would come to the office, flirt with me, and eye my breasts, not taking his eyes off of them the entire time he was there. I'd just let him look all he wanted too, and even made the view more available to him. This made Dan very jealous and after the salesman would leave, we'd fight, and then in our lust for each other, end up having sex, and it was the best sex ever, each time. We became more and more addicted to each other. The passion and zenith were indescribable.

Daniel repeatedly had to hire new deputies. People were only working out for a short time. A couple deputies were quoted as saying they quit because of our affair. They said they refused to work under such a lie as our relationship. Guess they thought it tainted the perception of the public's view of the sheriff's office. Yeah, right, like none of them had ever had a secret of their own. Dan just called them self-righteous, and let them go. There was always a new man waiting to be his deputy.

The next deputy he hired was Todd Raylord who spoke with a southern drawl. He seemed like a nice fellow. Todd was about my age, and we could relate on lots of subjects. Dan was twenty years older than me. He began to feel a little left out when Todd would visit with me about our generation. As I spoke with Todd, it made me want Dan more. I just couldn't get enough.

A few weeks after Todd started working for Dan, he asked me to come over to his and his friend's apartment for supper. Todd didn't actually know the full story of Dan and I yet. We hadn't let him into our confidence. I knew accepting his invitation would anger Dan, and I loved to fight with him, because the making up was so good. So I accepted and thought I'd make the odds a bit more interesting.

I went out and found Kathy and asked her to go with me. She accepted, and we went. Within a couple of hours of being at Todd's, Dan was knocking at his door. He looked very angry, and told me I could leave right now. Daniel kicked Kathy, called her a slut, and left with me, leaving Kathy behind at Todd's apartment. Once again proving I was under his skin, and counted more than his flesh and blood.

The sex was going to be great tonight and that's all I cared about. After all everything had always evolved around me and why should that stop now?

The next morning we were both in such a hurry to get ready for work. Daniel had stayed with me last night, and had to find some workable lie for Emily. It really didn't matter if Emily bought the excuse or not, it only mattered that he had one to give.

Our relationship was stressful and yet thrilling. I couldn't stop and I was counting on Dan not to stop either. Once again everything kept falling into place, as though it were part of some master plan. I convinced Dan and myself, that we were right, and that all our actions could be justified.

CHAPTER 9

*T*he finances were adding up. I lived in the beautiful home that we both had purchased, pining for the day when Daniel would move in with me for good. I flaunted my body and our relationship with Dan at every opportunity.

No one paid attention to Emily any longer. She just remained the washed up mess that she was. She took too many tranquilizers to even be in tune with life anymore. To watch her, and listen to her, would make a person sick. She often spoke of wishing Dan would die, and what she would do with his life insurance money. I think she really hated her husband now. Emily hated me also, although she was finally careful about what she said around me.

Time just continued to pass. Daniel would run for another election, it had been a long eight years. This next term caused a great concern and stress for our relationship. The town was mostly aware of our affair by now. This made Emily's and Daniel's being on the church board and community services, look foolish indeed. Dan lived such a double life. No one chose to confront us, or do anything to help Dan's family. Emily's neighbors saw us together all the time, but never told her. It was like they were just watching, waiting for the outcome, as if it were some television movie of the week.

Meanwhile, Daniel's kids all went to hell in a hand basket. Over these next few years as sheriff, Ann, Dan's oldest, stayed miles away at college, not acknowledging or seeing her parents much. I remember when Dan and I would take a prisoner to the State Penitentiary, which was just outside the city where Ann went to school. We would go out for dinner at various cafes, or restaurants in the area, but only a few times had we seen Ann. This put her in a difficult position, especially when we were kissing, and looked up to see her glaring at us. She didn't pay any attention to me, immediately moving toward her father, nodding her head as a greeting to him.

We became a little concerned when Emily announced Ann had called, and decided to come home for a visit. There was no holiday, or obvious reason why all of a sudden, she had decided to make a visit home. Daniel and I were sure it was because Ann was serious about telling her mother what she had seen going on with us.

Anticipating the worse, we waited to see what would happen. She would be home this coming weekend, and who knows what could take place.

In the meantime, I decided that there needed to be some fresh fighting going on between Dan and Emily. By the time Ann came home, Emily for sure would be the consistent mess that she had known most of her life.

I had a splendidly evil idea. Kathy had been living on the streets of Preston for quite some time. She only saw her parents once in a while. They had dismissed her, and thrown her aside never allowing her to move back home. Kathy was so trusting and unassuming, and being the sheriff's daughter, made her candy to the wrong element. She hung with the local drug crowd. Daniel hated this. It embarrassed him, the upstanding citizen he was. So he would snob her in public and barely speak to her at his home. I achieved what I had been after, Kathy's place. She hadn't been in her parents' home for months.

I went to Kathy and told her Ann was coming back for a visit. She wanted to see her sister Ann badly. With that seed planted, I went to

Emily and convinced her how wonderful it would be to have all her family together again.

Next, I had to work on Daniel. I told him he needed to fight all week with Emily, so she would be a nervous wreck when Ann got there. I made him realize that if he didn't, Emily might actually present her case to Ann, and Ann may help her see what was really going on, and jeopardize our life and the plans we had for it.

Once again I couldn't have dreamed such a perfect plan. I only had to wait for the drama to unfold and the weekend to blow over.

I invited myself to supper on Friday. I was hoping that seeing me there, would inhibit Ann from telling Emily about seeing her father and I at her college. All evening Ann stared at me, but she never volunteered the subject of us once. It was getting late, and I had to leave, so Daniel walked me to the door, and I left for home.

Saturday morning, Kathy showed up at her parents' house to see Ann. She'd only been there a short time, when Emily in her unknown hatred for Kathy began to argue with her. Ann could see the very reason she hated to come home to see her mother. Kathy hadn't done anything as usual. It just was a vengeance that Emily carried towards her.

Ann had asked her dad to keep Emily busy while she said goodbye to Kathy. Ann and Kathy left the living room and went into the kitchen to talk. Ann was looking for a snack in the refrigerator, and Kathy was standing beside her.

Without warning, Emily burst into the kitchen, out of jealousy, hatred, no one really knows for sure. She picked up a heavy table knife, swore at Kathy and threw the table knife directly at her. Kathy, knowing the knife was heading for her chest, turned around, facing her back to the on coming knife.

In a split second, Ann threw her arm out across Kathy's back. The knife landed blade first into Ann's arm on the inside part of her elbow. This moment seemed to last forever. Daniel couldn't believe his eyes. Did Emily really wish Kathy dead? Was she so sick to inflict such injury on a child of her own?

Immediately Emily ran to Ann's side apologizing over and over to her. She was saying she was sorry and meant the knife for Kathy. Then she sternly turned to Kathy and said, "See what you made me do to one of my favorite children. I hate you and always have."

Then Emily, Daniel and Ann left for the hospital. Kathy was left standing alone. Ann had six stitches that night and lied to the doctor about what had happened. Kathy and Ann wouldn't have a chance to talk about anything for years to come.

I was amazed when Dan told me just how deranged Emily had become. I also knew it would be to her demise eventually, and to my benefit.

Daniel and I were somewhat pleased about the weekend. Ann never brought up the subject to Emily about her father and I. We think she just gave up, and didn't want the trouble any longer.

From then on we always ran into her in the city, because Dan wanted to see her, but we talked about superficial things and she never spoke with us long.

Kathy begged Daniel one more time to help her. She had no where to live, she'd been living on the streets for a year now. She had been ganged raped at the local college in the men's dorm, during a party. This happened about a week after she left home, the night Emily knocked her out of a second story window. Too bad she had to experience sex for the first time in that way. The town labeled her a harlot and with no home of her own, she stayed from place to place often being raped or taken advantage of.

Daniel had noticed her one night sleeping on a park bench. The weather wasn't too bad, so he didn't let her know that he had seen her, and left her there, alone. Kathy was only nineteen, but still Dan couldn't focus on helping her. If he did, it would screw up our plans and my controls.

A few weeks after the incident when Ann was home, Kathy decided to run away with some guy who took an interest in her. I know she felt she had no other choice and she left.

It was always something.

CHAPTER 10

With Kathy gone, the months that followed just sweetened the pot. Emily was distraught, acting like she was grieving for a lost child. This girl she abused the entire time she was raising her, was now all of a sudden a missing child. She made me so ill. Dan stopped talking about Kathy as though she had died. His silence didn't bother me at all, because he was a quiet man anyway, and I was there to comfort him through it all.

The arguing between Daniel and Emily became worse, a matter of life and death. Emily wished Dan dead and fought with him in a heated rage. She became more physically violent than ever before. She actually tried to bust Dan's jaw again and hurt his old injury. Daniel couldn't sleep without keeping an eye out for Emily's wrath. She would attack him anytime, where ever possible.

I would come over some evenings and listen at the windows at Dan's request in case anything went wrong. One night when I was listening, it was the scariest thing I had ever seen or heard. Dan and Emily were punching each other. If Dan would try to walk away, Emily would jump on his back and bite him or twist his arms and head. She became so extreme that night, that she threatened Dan with an axe. They had a wood burning stove, and it was the axe they split kindling with. Emily threw it at Dan. He ducked and the axe missed him and landed in the wall paneling. In that moment I saw a look in Daniel's eyes, I hadn't seen before. He took the axe out of the wall and wrestled Emily to the floor, pinning her down. He raised the axe over her neck and said, "I'm going to kill you, you son-of-a-bitch," and then he laughed and laughed, an eerie laugh.

Emily just as angry and evil said, "Go ahead, kill me, and you can spend the rest of your life tortured in prison. I'd like that." Then Dan and Emily were quiet for a time. Daniel got off of Emily and put the axe back in the corner. The house was quiet for the rest of the night. The mood had been set.

Dan went on to win a third term in office. By the time he would finish being sheriff, he would have held that office for twelve years. He kept Emily as his wife for all that time. They'd been married almost thirty years by the end of this last term. Daniel and I would have been in a relationship for about 15 years.

He was a good sheriff and did his job well. There were times I was angry with him because he seemed to be married more to his job than any woman.

It was now more apparent than ever, that Emily was mentally ill and unpredictable. Whatever drove her over the edge was worth our attention. We had tried to make her be viewed by others as unstable for quite some time. She finally looked the ignorant monster we'd portrayed her to be.

These next four years were exhausting, but well worth my time. The first two years of this last term, Dan saw his youngest child finally finish high school. What a relief! They had all left home now. Emily continued to walk the streets every night like the lunatic she was. I loved what this all meant. One of the reasons Dan always gave me for not committing solely to me and leaving Emily was that he had to raise his children first. An admirable thought, but the hell those kids had been through made his motives ludicrous at best.

Still, I was taken care of, and living in a newly remodeled home, while his wife and family had and continued to live in an old dump. I was the one that could pull the strings to my puppets, these people whom I'd been controlling for years. I just once again bided my time. I would win, remember. I made drastic plans to make a move where Emily was concerned.

My best friend and I had a great time antagonizing and manipulating her. Neann Jo Worthing had been a friend to me for years. She was a radio dispatcher for a few years at the police station. She had gotten her husband the same way I had worked to get Dan. We had a lot in common. I could count on her to help me work out some of my plans.

It was to the point where Emily was following me all the time, and hanging around my house. I couldn't invite her in. I had pictures of Dan and the kids. They were all over my house, they were my family. No way could I explain that to her, nor did I want too. Besides she was crazy enough to kill me and I had much more living to do. I'd already taken her place over and over again. My obsession was far stronger than her irrational motives.

Neann saw her opportunity, and watched Emily, documenting every move she made. Eventually the evidence that we acquired, would put her in a mental hospital for the rest of her days if we were lucky. I couldn't wait to finally get her out of my way. People had started to complain about her, and something needed to be done. Town officials had spoken to Dan about the suspicious actions of Emily, and the complaints of people, who would look outside their windows at night to see her standing in their yards at strange hours. She was dubbed a menace to society, and like it or not, Daniel had to do something about it this time.

Emily was served a summons for court. There would be a public hearing on her mental status. No matter what she said, she wasn't able to talk her way out of her documented bad behavior. I watched for her that Monday morning. I really didn't care what happened to her, but as she passed the sheriff's office on her way to court, I wished her good luck. She glared at me, as if to wish me dead. Oh well, it would be a welcomed event to put her away.

During the hearing, Emily burst out at the judge. With all the evidence they already had against her, this was not good and seemed to be the judge's last straw. Finally the hearing was over. Emily was found mentally incompetent and placed under the state's care, to be committed to the state mental facility until, or if, she could ever be released into society again.

Unbelievable, I wanted to cheer, after all the years I'd put up with this woman's crap. Emily was now stripped of everything and a threat to no one. Dan, in a daze, was unsure what it all meant. You could see the dissolution in his expression. He'd get over it. I'd make sure of that.

"Good-bye Emily."

CHAPTER 11

*T*he hospital took Emily into custody right away. Daniel and I had to take her in the sheriff's car to the facility. This was part of our job as sheriff and deputy. I taunted her all the way to the hospital. She was very quiet and almost had an aura about her that was irrepressible. Eventually we had arrived at the hospital and pulled up the drive into the parking lot. Emily had said nothing for the entire two-hour trip. Before we got out of the car, I looked her straight in the eye and boastfully said, "Aren't you going to say anything before we leave you here?"

She had a distant look in the eyes as though she were miles away. I'll never forget what she said that day. "You played your game so well. I'll remember what you've done and you'll never forget me. We'll see each other again, Jill."

All the way back to Preston, I couldn't get her last and only words to me off my mind. Dan was still so very quiet. By the time we got back to town, he was smiling and visiting with me. We were realizing what we had planned for fifteen years. It couldn't have come too fast and for a moment, I almost forgot about the years it took to get to this point.

Dan and I focused more on each other now. It looked as though everything would work out for us. Could this be possible? After all this time waiting to complete the plan, was it now finished?

Another sheriff's election was to take place in about a month. We couldn't wait until November fourth. Hopefully Dan would win one more term as sheriff, divorce Emily and marry me. Sounded simple enough, but I wasn't going to count on that.

I helped him campaign, planning with him what we would do if he won or lost. As the day of the election drew closer, Dan had a feeling he would lose. He said he'd been approached by different people in the county and was told that because of what he'd done to his family, the town would no longer back him as sheriff.

Man! If blood could boil. Since when did this pious, self-righteous community all of a sudden care about the Royce children or Emily? It was all a huge slap in the face for Dan. He thought he'd lose the election for sure, so we just made our plans assuming he would no longer hold that job.

The election came and went. Dan did lose. He was sick about it, and went into a deep depression. I tried to get him to talk to me about it, but he wouldn't. He felt he'd lost all pride and stature. I was really concerned as to whether he would be all right or not. We'd been through so much together. How could I help him?

Dan dragged his feet for about a month, before I finally pressured him into moving in with me. I told him he needed to enjoy the home we had paid for and remodeled these past few years. He reluctantly gave in and we were now living in the same house, just the two of us.

I had to help make decisions for him for a while. He decided to divorce Emily, stating it was because of her mental illness. She got nothing for all those years of marriage. Dan on the other hand at least had the house he'd raised their kids in and could do what he wanted with it. He chose to rent it out.

The house provided a kind of therapy. He would go there all day and work on remodeling it the way he was supposed to, when his kids were growing up.

I'd often find him by himself in a room working as if nothing else mattered. At the end of my quest for the perfect man, I now had a sad and broken one. Well no matter how it all looked, I had won and I was still obsessed with this man and the passion I carried for him.

Finally the divorce was final and it took three months of persistent nagging to get Dan to say he would marry me. This was all I ever wanted. I was thirty-six and had never been married, obviously because of our love affair. I was so excited. I was going to be Mrs. Daniel Royce. His kids were out of the picture. His wife was gone and put away. What more could I want? What more could there be?

CHAPTER 12

❀

*N*eann began to help me plan the wedding. It had to be with all the trimmings. I deserved it. Should I wear white? Could I be brazen enough to pull it off? Then I saw the most lovely light blue dress. I was a little heavier than I used to be and this dress would help hide the weight. We would have a simple ceremony at the Christian Church we were going to at that time.

Dan's kids were all out of town. I convinced Daniel that they shouldn't be invited or contacted, until the wedding was over in case they didn't approve. We didn't need any more interference. Everything went well, the flowers, guests, reception, it was all perfect, just the way I had imagined it.

How could I forget the trauma, hurt and evil that kept our relationship afloat? None of it mattered now, as Daniel made his commitment to me legal. I needed to forgot all the events that had led up to this wedding, just for this one day. We were married and all on lookers watched in a form of amazement to see us. It was my day, and I would savor it forever.

The week passed by and we had a small honeymoon. Then it was back to reality. I still worked as a deputy and a secretary for the sheriff's office, and Dan had no job. It was a difficult circumstance for Dan. He'd always had a job all his life. He was certainly depressed to say the least. I insisted he had to find something to keep his days busy, and that he couldn't retire yet. Dan was in his late fifties and jobs that paid anything were hard to get at that age. Nevertheless, he had to find one and not only because he needed something to do, but for our spending appetite as well. He applied for a few jobs. It took him almost a month after we were married to be hired.

Finally one job came through. Daniel was hired at a tea-pot making company. The company was called Matic Tea, and was just down the street from where we lived. Dan was tired and didn't seem to want this job necessarily, but he never confided all his feelings to anyone anyway. Daniel kept his mouth shut and worked the job. It felt good to get over that hurdle.

Problems, that's an understatement. When Dan's kids found out he'd married me, all hell broke loose. We received phone calls and letters from them stating everything from disgust, to the least we could have done was to tell them. These letters from Dan's kids really hurt him. They didn't phase me at all. Dan didn't know how to talk to his children anyway. His kids felt abandoned by him. His daughter, Kathy, did write him a letter. She simply told Dan that whatever he'd done, he was her father and she thought he should keep his relationship with his children and grandchildren.

The first couple of years, things seemed so peaceful, like we'd achieved our earliest dreams for our lives. There were no ex-wifes with alimony payments, or child support payments to make. The timing was perfect. We had everything, new cars, furnishings, clothing, there was no one else to buy for or be concerned with. It was mine, mine, mine, and Daniel's, too, of course. Whenever we wanted something, we just pulled out a credit card and it was ours. It was so convenient and affordable for us. We purchased a mobile camper to travel around the country in. In the summer we'd pick up and go to Montana or some other beautiful place and just camp for a week or two. We were always glad though, to get back home to our little house. It was our foundation.

I continued to gain weight throughout this marriage. At one point, I was over two hundred and sixty pounds, as big as Dan's ex-wife Emily once was. It didn't bother me though, I knew I had a firm lock on Dan's and my life. After all, I could place him at the home of Malaine the night she died, in his first term as sheriff. I know that fact in itself kept Daniel in line. Plus all the slightly illegal tricks we pulled on Emily and others. The point was it had always been Dan's foremost concern that he looked upright, and took pride in who he was and what others thought of him. To expose such dirty dealings would bring him down, and destroy his law enforcement career. It was what his peers thought that mattered in its own ironic way. Dan thrived on public approval.

CHAPTER 13

*T*here were times such as holidays and vacations where Dan and I would visit his children and grandchildren. I almost forgot myself. I started to fit in with them, finding I had a need for acceptance in his family. His kids were hospitable to me and sometimes acted as though they cared for me. I liked that and started to care some for them also.

A few years had passed and we'd been married four years now. Emily was released from the mental institution a year ago. She had never contacted us or bothered us. The kids said they never heard much from her, but when they did she brought up a lot of old unfinished business. Emily seemed to thrive on the thought of revenge against me. She would always blame, and hate me for stealing her husband and family. I felt she was basically harmless as long as we didn't have contact. Outside of an occasional strange phone call where no one would speak, Dan and I tried to push her out of our minds. We ignored her presence or any acknowledgement of her.

Life did feel good. Daniel had gained a lot of self-esteem back from not being sheriff any longer. In fact, the new sheriff and county officials would come to him for law knowledge and advise on different cases and prisoners. Daniel was very keen on his state and federal law, and had been sheriff for twelve years, so his experience was of value to his old co-workers. The police chief and highway patrol officers, who sometimes were rivals with Dan, were now seeking his knowledge on their toughest cases. There was strength in friendship between them. Daniel felt he once again was involved in active law enforcement. This made him happy.

A few times throughout our marriage, Dan's kids needed help financially, but no matter what amount it was, I always made him say no. These weren't my kids and though I'd known them while they grew up, and about the hard life they'd had, it wasn't my problem. Even when Dan saved money with me all those years and we took it from his children and family to make our future lifestyle, that didn't matter now. Our money was ours, and I just refused it to them. Dan and I did have words when I caught him giving twenty dollars to Kathy, who said she needed food for her kids. In any case his kids stopped asking for help of any kind, and got the message.

I felt pretty clever. Dan was working on restoring old cars, besides his job. I was still top dog at work in the sheriff's office. No one knew that system or computer like I did, and they needed me. Life was great! I'm telling you, top of the world, not to mention I wore the name of Daniel Royce so proudly and flaunted it wherever I could. There was still something intriguing about being the other woman who won.

We were actually financially sound. I didn't have to think where I spent the money, or used the credit cards. I could buy anything I wanted. I just wanted more. There was always room for more. Daniel had a large company fund when he left the sheriff's job. Plus, some great insurance polices, and pension plans. We had money, but kept it to ourselves.

We found a rewarding insurance policy that would pay one million dollars, should Dan die. I felt we needed one more life insurance policy. I convinced Dan that he should get this one. After all he was twenty years older than me. If he were to die suddenly, how would I keep up the lifestyle I had become accustomed to living? He surely wouldn't expect me to live any other way. Reluctantly, Dan decided in favor of buying the policy. That was a relief off of my mind.

I had everyone and everything just where I wanted it. I was glad I'd taken control of every area of my life strategically speaking. It looked as though I'd accomplished exactly what I'd charted for. I never wondered how long it would last. I could keep control, nothing to it.

Dan and I bought a couple of old houses in town to use as rentals. They needed some fixing up to make them livable for tenants, but Dan could dry wall and remodel, saving us a lot of money and making the homes a reasonable, sound investment. Rent money for us would be sheer profit. Daniel worked hard on the houses and within a few weeks, we were able to rent them.

After the second house was finished being dry walled and cleaned, Dan suddenly became very ill. He was throwing up, and had severe constant pain in his chest and a painful cough. I hadn't seen him so sick before. He insisted it must have been from dry walling without a mask on his face. Maybe he had breathed too much of the dust into his lungs. In a few days, he was worse and in pain from his coughing.

We made an appointment for him with our doctor. It was about a week before we could get him into the clinic. Dan was so sick. I felt somewhat sorry for him, but he'd be ok, everything always was. Why would it be any different now?

CHAPTER 14

*A*s soon as we could get Dan to the doctor, I knew it would be just fine. We had to plan our anniversary party in a few days, we'd been married for five years now. I had a lot to do. We were to have a huge party with all our friends. The doctor kept Dan most of the day, running numerous tests on him to be sure of what was wrong. This was a Monday, but the test results wouldn't be back until Thursday afternoon, that seemed fine. Dan was pretty confident he'd be well, and our party was still planned for Friday. We'd just go ahead with the preparations for it.

The week went by, Daniel got over his cough, enough to go to work anyway. Our week went on as usual, hoping for the best. Then on Thursday we went to Dan's doctor appointment to find out the results of his tests. Our doctor was overly kind as he brought us into his office. He had us sit down and then he went on to explain what they'd found.

"Dan," he said, "there's no easy way to tell you this, but we are sure of our findings." He then stated that Dan had a metastatic disease found in his bone scan. He explained that meant Daniel had progressive, non-small cell lung cancer, carcinoma in his left lung, which had caused nerve involvement that would lead to paralysis of his vocal cords. His voice had been hoarse for a while now, but we thought it was only because he was sick, we had no idea it could be permanent. The doctor told us he might never regain his full range of voice again.

We both smoke constantly. I guess Daniel had been smoking for over forty years. I was surprised. Dan answered the nurse's questions for his paper work. He said he'd been a greater than eighty pack a year smoker for quite sometime. You know, we never counted packs, or thought about smoking much, we just lit up and enjoyed a smoke, our vice, I guess. But now it sounded as if smoking was going to squeeze the last breath out of Dan. The doctor said it was serious, and all they could do was surgery to see how bad the cancer had spread, and if it could be stopped in time to save Dan's life.

I was totally speechless on the way home. There was a dead silence between us. Dan had cancer and it didn't look promising at all. Tomorrow was our anniversary party. We couldn't cancel now. It was too late to let everyone know. Besides we needed something happy to take the burden of this off our minds.

The doctor called us back on Friday afternoon, and told us he had scheduled Dan for surgery on Monday morning. He explained the surgery to us. They would cut Dan's body from the chest around the ribs into the back. Then they would twist his body like a biscuit can, and that way get a better view of the entire lung. If it was just in the left lung as they thought, then they could remove that lung, at the same time, removing the cancer. If that were the case, Daniel would need radiation treatment for a while, eventually being in remission or cancer free. That was the best we could hope for. The worst being the cancer had spread and there was no hope.

Hanging up the phone, Daniel began to cry. I'd never seen him cry, except when he spoke of his mother who had died when he was eight years old. He was trembling. I tried to comfort him, but wasn't much help. He was far away in his own thoughts. That night our house was extremely sad and quiet.

Friday morning came and it was the day of our anniversary party. Daniel seemed in good spirits, after sleeping all night. All the bad news about his health was like a horrible dream. It couldn't be true. We both decided that the doctors were going to find the best, and that he would be fine.

The evening arrived, all our friends came over and we had good food, games, and pleasant conversation. It was fun and after what we'd been through these last few days with Dan's health, fun was what we needed.

Monday came quickly for us. We met our doctor in Capital City at the university hospital. It was extremely advanced in cancer treatments and surgeries of this nature. They prepared Dan for surgery, and I waited for six hours before surgery was over, then another three hours to see Dan because he was in intensive care that long. During the time he was in intensive care, the doctor came and spoke with me. He said he was very sorry, but they had found that the cancer had spread outside the lung, and was embedded into the lining of both lungs. They wanted to give Dan a very potent radiation treatment. It was thought that this might slow the cancer down. They gave Dan less that a year to live, especially without the treatment.

Finally Daniel awoke. He was quick to ask about his surgery and what they'd found. I immediately called for the doctor and nurse. I didn't want to tell him, so I avoided doing so. The doctor came in, he told Dan everything, just as he had told me earlier. Dan sank down in his bed. He couldn't believe what he was hearing. He had been on Prozac medication for chronic depression for a few years now. Soon he'd be taking large quantities of morphine for the cancer pain. He was so overwhelmed. What could I do? Nothing, he had to suffer this problem alone. I couldn't make it go away, even if I'd wanted too.

I sat with him all day in the hospital. Finally it grew late, it had been a long, lonely day and I could face no more. Daniel had cried himself to sleep and I needed sleep too.

I left, thinking alone in the car as I drove back home. This just couldn't be happening. There had to be a way out of this tragedy. I actually cried, the thought of being without him after all these years was suddenly devastating.

CHAPTER 15

*D*an was kept in the hospital almost two weeks after the strong radiation session he needed. During that time, he was enrolled in hospice services. When he did come home, they came to the house each day and helped him while I was at work. They seemed to be of help in cheering him up. I think it was just another face, and person to chat with for him, when I wasn't there. We tried to put all the horrors aside, and get life back to a normal routine.

Dan no longer worked. He was home permanently now. The strong pellet radiation treatment had taken its toll on him. The doctor's reports read that Daniel was upon examination a thin, cachectic, chronically ill gentleman, who actually appeared to be older than his chronologic age. He also had much difficulty in swallowing and trouble with breathing. Dan said he felt like he could never get enough air to breathe. In any case, life as we had known it, would never be normal again. Daniel lost more of his voice after the pellet treatment. He now spoke in a whisper and always would from this time forward.

Dan knew he had to be strong and work through this situation. He started regular radiation treatment. He went every day for two hours at the hospital. It took a lot out of him. He was weak and weary, often not talking much for days at a time. His appetite wasn't very good anymore. He said that after that major radiation treatment, he couldn't taste food. Everything he ate tasted burnt, and his food was never delicious like it used to be. When he started to lose weight rapidly, the doctors became extremely concerned. They examined Dan and asked him about his eating habits. I guess he told them, he had trouble swallowing, and couldn't get much food down.

Because of this problem the doctor decided to put a feeding tube in Daniel's stomach, and from that time on he would be fed liquid nourishment in that tube. He could only have ice chips and hard candy to suck on. This would be the way he would eat until he died. He would never again taste his favorite supper of hamburgers on the grill, or pork and beans and fried potatoes. He had lost the privilege of enjoying and tasting food. Everything was certainly more of a task for him now. The simplest things were an extra effort. I really did feel sorry for him, but the depression was overwhelming me, in a suffocating manner.

At hospice request, we purchased a hospital bed to be placed in our little home. We put it right in the living room, where the couch had been. A hospital bed in my front room. It seemed annoying and in the way. I tried to keep my perspective, that a man was dying and needed his last comforts.

We had no contact sexually at all since Dan's operation. It had been months now. I continued to press Daniel for intercourse of some kind. I told him that he should still try at least to satisfy me. We had several arguments over sex, but I always got him to do something for me no matter how he felt. He seemed to fade farther and farther away from me.

I grew tired of taking care of him everyday when I got home from work. We fought all the time, me using more words, and Dan persisting in quiet as usual.

His children would come as often as each could, to visit him. He enjoyed them, but it irritated me because he didn't prefer my company any longer. Most of the kids couldn't see Dan all the time. Brian however came every weekend to see his dad. Brian became the buffer and go between for the other kids.

Dan was concerned that all the legal matters were in my hands. He asked me to make an appointment with our attorney, making sure that his kids were left a decent amount of his estate. I always put this off. I was to get everything, and there was no way in hell that I was going to share it. Dan made me promise that upon his death, I would make sure his kids got an inheritance. He didn't want a repeat of what his father had done to him and his siblings. His father had remarried and the stepmother took everything when Dan's father died, giving the children nothing, plus made all their lives a living hell in the process. Even though I promised Dan, I could have gave a shit less, but knew he would never know anyway. He'd be dead.

I would sell the house the Royce children grew up in, and pay off the house we were living in. I also wanted to pay all our credit cards off so I could start on them again. Then I'd still be collecting rent on the rentals we owned. I'd get Dan's pension money, sheriff's benefits, and life insurance from two polices, and veteran's pay. When this was all over, I stood to gain lofty profits in all financial areas.

Dan was extremely unhappy at home with me. His daughter, Kathy, and he had developed a special friendship over the phone. She would call him everyday and visit with him. He told her and the other kids he was sorry for what he'd done to their family, by having an affair with me and letting their care go. He asked them to forgive him and they seemed to do that.

Where'd that leave me? All of a sudden I felt like such a harlot, seductress, worthless. How dare he be sorry, and voice remorse over our affair. Torrid as it was, he had played his part well. We just continued to drift apart.

CHAPTER 16

*I*t had now been several months of dealing with Dan and his cancer. He was fading fast. His kids had been away for over a week, and wouldn't get back to see him for a two week span. Dan was irritated because he enjoyed their visits, but he wasn't angry with them and tried to understand. He sure didn't apply that understanding to me any longer.

I, on the other hand, had been busy working on planning Daniel's funeral, and it was to be an elaborate sending off. I tried to have detailed plans of what Dan had said he wanted. We needed an expensive cherry wood casket, his shoes on, his black suit, a steel vault for burial, hymns of his choice etc. I didn't tell him, but I had even planned to place a peppermint candy in his folded hands, since it was his favorite candy and he always carried a bag of them around with him. I was caught up in his death and getting finished with all this mess. I made an appointment with the local funeral home. I told the owner of the funeral home that Dan and I needed to come in and pick out his casket.

The funeral director insisted it was not reasonable for Dan to have this burden. He said that since I knew what Daniel wanted, we could pick it out for him and make the arrangements ourselves.

Being bold, I proceeded to have it done my way. Even though I had to push Dan to go, I got my point across and he went with me.

The funeral director was agape when we entered the office. You could tell he felt uncomfortable with Dan there, almost as if he were really concerned about Daniel's feelings. Oh please! The funeral home would profit from such an expensive funeral. I didn't feel like I could get away with a cheap one. Dan had a lot of life insurance, and he had been the town's sheriff for twelve years. Besides, Brian, Dan's son and I were having a fairly decent relationship and since he was to be the executor of my will after Dan died, even though I planned for him and his siblings to receive nothing, I still had to keep up appearances.

As the funeral director explained the details of Daniel's funeral, he was so quiet. He would crack a smile once or twice at the remarks of the director, trying to relieve the tension. The visit was almost over, and seemed to go better than I expected. "Ok, follow me," the director said, "and we'll pick out the casket." I could hear Dan take a deep breath. We all stood up and were led out of the office into an upstairs room.

The room was the size of a ballroom. It was decorated nicely with beautiful caskets displayed from one end of the room to the next. As we moved from casket to casket and listened to the detailed explanations of each, things seemed to be moving right along.

All of a sudden, Dan let out a loud cry, and threw up all over the floor in the display room. I was stunned. I couldn't believe he did that. Immediately the funeral director and his associates helped Daniel, and got him cleaned up. They just helped Dan to our car, and placed him in the back seat to rest.

When the funeral director came back into his office, I apologized for the incident. He glared at me and yelled, telling me he had told me that bringing someone in Dan's condition, to buy a casket was cruel and not a good idea. I tried to calm him down, as I still needed to pick out a casket. We went back up stairs and I just picked the cherry wood one we'd both looked at first.

It took about another hour to finish all the arrangements. I suppose I should have taken Dan home, but the wait didn't hurt him. After all, that's all his life was now, waiting. Finally I was finished. I got in the car and drove us home.

When we got inside the house, Dan told me he hadn't wanted to go, and he wouldn't have gotten sick again, if I'd just left him at home.

You know, I said, "I've just about had it with feeding you through a tube and nursing you when I know you're going to die soon. Watching you slowly die hasn't been a treat for me you know. If you want me to continue to take care of you, shut up. For a moment I felt pretty cocky, but the next minute I felt awful. "I'm sorry Dan."

It doesn't matter, Jill," he said, "we don't love each other any longer, and I regret my decisions in life."

Oh! I was so angry he said that. I started to say to him, you regret…"

"Yes Jill," he spoke, "I'm calling the hospital, and hospice is helping pay for me to live there until I die."

"Well you can't," I screamed out.

The next day, hospice picked Dan up and he was gone from our house. Part of me felt sad, but there was a burden removed, now that he wasn't in my care any longer. I visited him once or twice a day. Dan was always under so much medication. He'd fade in and out of our conversations.

Every day he would ask me to please bring the lawyer of our estate to see him so we could go over it, and assure his children would receive something. He'd plead for me to be fair with them, and allow them an inheritance.

I'd usually have an excuse as to why our attorney couldn't come, but I reassured Dan that I would take care of it. Our attorney was Flip London. He was a crafty fellow and worked right with me for his share, too.

Dan became really insistent on voicing his estate concerns around others. He was angry that I hadn't done what he'd asked me to do. I informed him of our sickest secret together, the death of Malaine Rabinski. I told him he would be quiet and die as such, or that I would sing loud and make him out to be the killer in that situation. I let him know that no one would believe him or feel sorry for him. Dan knew I would blacken his good name and he couldn't stand for that. He still had some illusion of his integrity that he had to hang on to. From that day on, we never spoke of estate matters, or anything else about the will.

Though Daniel hardly spoke to me, I continued to go and visit him each day. I would just sit with him. He slept a lot now, and was increasing morphine dosages all the time for the pain.

Daniel would wake up every so often sometimes saying, "Do you see that man outside my window?"

I could never see anyone there. Then Dan would say the man outside his window was waiting for him to take him home to God because God had forgiven him for all the wrong he'd done. I'd just ignored him until he'd dose off again.

Brian just humored his father, because the man Daniel seemed to see outside his window, for some reason gave him peace.

I was curious of spiritual things, and truly wanted to see Daniel take his last breath. I thrived on it now. I went to the hospital all I could because the doctors all agreed it wouldn't be long before he died. Death didn't scare me. I wasn't going to die.

I'll always be angry about the day Dan died though. I was there, I saw him, but he didn't talk much. He asked me to leave to go to the store to buy new batteries for his tape player. He said he loved to listen to his favorite music. That was all he could do now. So I left, and Damn it, while I was gone, he died.

It was my responsibility to call everyone and tell them, that Dan had passed away. When I called Brian he said he had to speak with me right away. He was upset and I felt compelled to meet with him.

When we met, he pulled a paper from his pocket and fumbled it between his fingers. Seeming nervous, he said, "Jill, my Uncle DeMond gave this note to me. He said it was written by my father and that my dad shoved this in his hand the last time he visited with him." Brian began to read the note.

∽

Brian, Please, please make Jill be fair about my estate with all my children. She promised me she would, hold her to that promise.

Dad

This was disturbing. Think, I told myself. "Oh, Brian, it's alright. I promised your dad I would make an appointment with our attorney Flip London, and have you be made the executor of my will, now that your dad is no longer here. Don't worry, I'll take care of it all. I would never cheat you kids."

I almost had to pinch myself. I sounded so convincing. However this seemed to pacify Brian, and besides there was nothing he and his siblings could do short of a huge costly court suing. I just didn't count on that at all. Taking advantage during people's grief was after all, my specialty. I'd be living real well on the remainder of their dad's money.

The day of the funeral arrived. It went just as planned. Everyone showed up except Dan's daughter, Kathy. Kathy stayed away from Preston for her own safety. Then without telling anyone her plans, she showed up at the visitation unexpected. I ran up to hug her. With a huge smile on my face and told her that I was glad she could come. I hadn't seen her in quite a while.

Kathy stepped back. She looked gruffly at me, and as I tried to hug her, she spoke softly in my ear. "Jill, she said, I hope you've learned your lesson and that you don't ever do this to any one else's family again."

Without thinking, I answered her, saying, "I won't." Then she moved away from me. She meant, of course, the affair. I followed her and told her that the entire funeral was going to be video taped and asked her if she'd like a copy. She just stood there and glared at me. She declined my offer, and said she thought it was rude to exploit a person's death by video taping it, but that it was no surprise to her that I wanted to.

Kathy didn't stay for the funeral. Her brother Brian had taken her out to see the grave-site, but the stone wasn't up yet. I told her I would send her a picture of the grave when the stone was put up.

Her response, "Whatever, Jill."

It was the day of the funeral, and I was ready to be through with all of this. Everything was going as scheduled. The head stone had been purchased weeks before. It was a large stone, made of marble, with Dan's name on one side and mine on the other, an impressive head stone. The pallbearers were Terri Yenn, Mick Worthing, Flip London, and a few other men who had worked with Dan during his law enforcement career.

All in all, the funeral went smooth and was quickly over. It was all over now. Everything was mine.

CHAPTER 17

When everyone finally left, I had to have a stiff drink. I had a bottle of whiskey. I knew getting drunk would be the best thing to do.

I spent a few days trying to go through my grief. There were some good times for Dan and I. I had to work through this past year of hurt feelings in our relationship. A lot needed to be accomplished these next weeks to come, with the will and life insurance policies, etc. Dan's insurance had paid all medical bills upon his death. That was a terrific relief. The last couple of months that Dan was in the hospital, I had looked for job opportunities away from Preston. For years Daniel had pleaded for me to quit working for the sheriff's department. Especially after he lost the last election. I couldn't do it, I stuck to my guns, the money was too good, and I was familiar with, and settled in my job.

I didn't want to move from this town. I needed to flaunt my success of being Mrs. Daniel Royce. Now, I had the money to live wherever I wished, and I was going places.

Brian met me at Mr. London's law office, to become the executor of his father's will. I inherited everything with the feeble promise of it all one day going to Dan's kids. This was much more than I'd hoped for. I planned on spending it all. One thing I did very well at was spending money, anybody's money.

I quickly sold the house on Kaple street that Dan and Emily had raised their kids in. I'm sure the kids thought, surely I'd give them that money. No way! I got twenty-five thousand for the old dump, and paid off my mortgage with it. It was just a piece of shit real estate to me.

Since none of Dan's children fought me in court over it, I went on to pursue all the big spending thrills of the enormous life insurance policies I was to cash in on. I believe Kathy would have fought me, only her siblings had no understanding of how I had screwed them, and she was so worn out from her parents' abuse and the divorce she had just gone through, that she stood alone and just went on. So much insurance, I was so clever. A new door had opened for me, and I was ready to walk through it.

I did find that new job. It was in Chicago at a large computer technologies firm. I was making the move to Chicago and with this new job, life would be great. It seemed that my sorrows and struggles with Dan were over now. Of course I kept the rental properties that we purchased in Preston. I profited a tidy sum of money from them each month. I guess I knew I'd always had it in me to live spoiled and wealthy given half a chance. There was so much to look forward to. Dan wasn't here. What a sigh of relief I felt. No one to care for or take care of, just me.

I wanted to straighten out some personal affairs since I was moving to Chicago soon. My adoptive mother was quite elderly, and I made sure she signed me over the power of attorney, giving me sole ownership of all she had, should she die while I was away.

She did die, a few months after I moved. In fact, it was the easiest funeral ever for me. I'd already buried my adopted father years ago, he died eleven years to the date of Daniel's death, and was buried on the same day eleven years earlier than Dan.

As far as the only mother I'd ever known, she was such a bitch to grow up with and often locked me in a dark closet for hours, when she was angry. I was glad she was gone. I didn't have to think about these people any longer. They were all dead.

It actually feels as though several years have gone by since Daniel died. Remarkably it's only been a short time. Things have changed so much. I don't keep in touch even with Brian anymore, or any of Dan's kids. Kathy cut ties with me right after Dan's funeral. Ann never contacts me, and the youngest one sends the occasional Christmas card. Just as well, I have nothing to say to any of them, and nothing I want to give them.

Life just keeps getting better. Today at a work gathering through a co-worker, I met Jonah Day. At first he didn't appeal to me at all. He was at least ten years older than I was. Dan had been twenty years older. Jonah's personality shone more than his looks, probably, because he was a plain looking man. I wasn't getting any younger, and I started to involve myself with him.

Jonah soon asked me to marry him. I'd checked on him through all my past connections in law enforcement. He had worked as a sanitation worker for the past twenty years, and stood to gain a hefty pension, and retirement benefits. I'd never given much thought to marrying a trash man, but if the price was right, it could work.

This guy had no idea, with whom he was dealing. He had no children to share his wealth. What a perfect set up. I found that Jonah had a high risk of heart attack. This was no concern to me, except that I might inherit his money faster.

I pursued the wedding. Again my friend, Neann, helped me plan the event. We got married in Preston, at the same Christian church that Daniel and I had been married in. In fact the same minister Reverend Perell married Jonah and I even. I thought about Daniel throughout the entire service, fantasizing that it was Dan I was marrying, and that he wasn't dead.

Reality soon set in. Jonah and I were on our honeymoon now, and it wasn't Dan I was in bed with, and the sex wasn't as good either.

I had to keep focused on my goals and where Jonah fit into them. I couldn't let him know what I was really thinking or much about me at all. My reasoning had told me not to be afraid of this remarrying. I had craftily worked so intensely on becoming Mrs. Daniel Royce. I just couldn't give up that Royce name. So from that day forward, I was known as Jill Royce Day. I continued my friendships in Preston, and felt proud of myself, no matter if anyone else did or not.

Jonah and I had been married almost three years when he had a fatal heart attack and died at home. I luckily wasn't home at the time. Although the doctor said it was unfortunate for Jonah, because I could have helped him. If the emergency workers had just gotten there a few minutes earlier, they may have been able to save him. Since he was alone and no one could get to him soon enough, he died.

Unbelievable, this would be my fourth funeral that I had the controls over in approximately twenty years. This would not be complicated and I was glad of that. I buried Jonah and since he didn't really have any family to speak of, except a sister he'd disowned years ago, there was no one to contact.

Finally he was gone and that burden was off my shoulders. I was no worse off. It was only a marriage of convenience anyway.

A few months passed, still I was wealthy and my cash flow was great. I never had changed that will of mine. I'd still left Dan's son on it as executor. I didn't plan on having anything left when I died. I was living an excellent life and spending the money just fine.

CHAPTER 18

Since everything kept moving right along for me, I didn't give the past much thought. Then one day the past found me, and it was lying on my kitchen table. I'd received a letter in the mail today that stated: Ms. Sterns, (Royce-Day);

We are having an inquisition into the death of Malaine Rabinski. At the request of her family and unfinished business in the previous investigation, we the investigative council, seek to re-open the case and subject it to trial if necessary.

The body will be exhumed and studied for evidence missed and subsequently lead to a murder suspect, that justice might ultimately be served in this case. You will be contacted soon about your involvement.

The Office of District Court Judge
David Albine

Oh my God! How could this be happening? That woman died over twenty years ago. Dan assured me he had wiped out all mention of it in our law records. Now he was gone and I was going to have to face this alone.

Just then the door-bell rang. I'd heard it many times before, but it scared the hell out of me because of its eerie timing. I answered it slowly, still in shock.

"Are you Jill Royce Day?" a plain clothed man asked me. "Yes, that's me."

He then shoved a paper in my hand. It was a summons to appear in Preston, a week from today at the Onion County court house, for the re-opening of the case of Malaine Rabinski's death. I felt a panic, unlike I'd never felt before. What? How? Who had the lists of suspects, and why was it coming out now? I didn't forget that Dan and I were next to the top of the list. Of course there were others, her lover Bob Wolfe and who could forget Emily and her anger that night. But Bob Wolfe had just died last year, and Dan was dead, and Emily was God knows where. The chief of police was retired and since had been able to clear himself from this matter. Besides, I was one of the top suspects. What to do? I needed a lawyer right away. My head was spinning. It was going to be a hell of a week waiting to appear in court for this inquiry. It couldn't come soon enough, yet I wished it wasn't to be at all.

The week passed and I made the trip to Preston. There it was the law center I'd been in so many times before as a secretary, and deputy sheriff under Daniel's terms. It was an unnerving feeling, like stepping back into another time. As I entered the court room, I noticed it was filled to capacity with people. I took my place next to Flip my attorney.

The prosecutor gave a summary of events leading up to Malaine's death. He spoke of her achievements, and how she had graduated from college, the top of her class. He went on to say, She had a promising career as a paralegal. Then her life was stolen from her. Although her personal life may show she did not use discretion in choosing to have an adulteress affair with the former county attorney, who has since passed on. She still did not deserve to be snuffed out, if you will, and then the criteria of justice never met. We, the prosecution, intend to prove beyond a reasonable doubt, that there was indeed foul play in the death of Malaine Rabinski, and that justice still counts more than two decades after the crime. The scales of justice must balance, and it is you ladies and gentlemen of the court who must balance them. We the prosecution call Jill Royce Day as our first witness.

Upon taking the oath, I took the witness stand. My mind was racing, and staying focused was extremely hard. I knew I had to be collected or blow the whole caper. I was so full of fear. My attorney, Flip London, was there and I knew him always to be crafty where needed, although I never let anyone be in full control of me or my destiny. The prosecuting attorney then established who I was and how I knew Malaine. He also brought Daniel as the acting sheriff of that time, in on the story. Of course going on to exploit the adulteress affair we had during that time frame. All through the examination, I had no excuses, no reasons, and the less I tried to defend our actions the safer I felt with my testimony.

Prosecuting Attorney (PA)
Jill
Defense Attorney (DA)

(PA): Are you a jealous person Jill?
Jill: Oh no, (I answered before thinking. Of course I was jealous and everyone in that town knew it anyway.)
(PA): Are you sure you wouldn't like to rephrase your answer?
Jill: Sure, I can be jealous if the situation calls for it.
(PA): Did you know Malaine Rabinski?
Jill: Yes.
(PA): Were you friends with her?
Jill: No.
(PA): Why not?
Jill: The occasion never arose to be.
(PA): You were just co-workers for the same law-enforcement team, right?
Jill: Co-workers, yes.
(PA): Were you ever at Malaine's house?

Jill: (She gives no answer)

(PA): I'll state the question again. Were you ever at Malaine Rabinski's house?

Jill: Yes.

(PA): Yes, when would that have been?

Jill: The night she died. (Wow! You could have heard a pin drop. An object came flying out of Flip's mouth. My attorney had suddenly woke up.) "I object," he stated, "the witness hasn't been charged with any crime. She is simply here for information in this case."

(PA): Your honor I am only trying to establish the whereabouts of Ms. Day, the night of Malaine's death.

Judge: Objection over ruled.

Jill: I decided that I could convince myself it wasn't me that killed Malaine, therefore I should tell all the truth I knew. (Something deep inside me told me they were going to find the truth anyway and catch any lies.)

(PA): Let's go through the formalities: Malaine Rabinski, born December eighteenth, nineteen thirty-four and died November twenty-eighth, nineteen seventy-three of suffocation. She is buried in the Graceland cemetery, just a few feet north of the sundial. She had no prior history of lung or respiratory problems. There was no reason for her to stop breathing or to suffocate. Thirty-nine years old, such promise gone. Now Jill, if I may call you Jill?

Jill: (nodded yes.)

(PA): Why were you at Malaine's home on the night she died?

(DA): I object. As Ms. Day's attorney, I have to stop this line of questioning. This is an inquiry as to the death of Malaine Rabinski. It is a step in finding who is responsible if anyone for her death. My client has not thus been charged with this pretentious crime and therefore hasn't had time to prepare a case for herself. I ask for time with my client before any further questioning can take place. To find the truth for one life lost, we must also give due process to those lives present.

Judge: Will both attorneys please approach the bench?

(PA): You honor we feel as new evidence per questioning today, we have enough to hold Jill Royce Day at least on suspicion of murder in the third degree.

(DA): I object, your honor. Jill is not on trial here.

(PA): Again, your honor. This woman has admitted she was at the home of the murder victim the night she died. Ms. Royce Day was possibly one of the last people to see Malaine alive. She must know more.

Judge: I believe you need to get this case in order. We will adjourn for today and you both must proceed accordingly. Court is adjourned.

The day had consisted of badgering from one attorney to another. Questions! Questions! I couldn't take anymore. Finally, it was over, at least for today. I thought about the day and wondered what the officials would make of it.

As I was leaving the law center, a sheriff's deputy approached me.

"Jill," he said. I turned around to answer him. Just as I did, he slapped a handcuff on my left wrist. "You are under arrest for the murder of Malaine Rabinski," he informed me. Then he went on to read me my rights as he handcuffed my right wrist also.

I was in shock. My attorney was just coming out the door. He stopped and told me he'd meet us at the jail to negotiate a bond release. There I was, on my way to jail.

CHAPTER 19

*F*lip worked for hours trying to get a bondsman and work out my bond. You wouldn't have thought it should have been so hard. After all, I was a sheriff's deputy for this county for over twelve years. I just couldn't comprehend what the delay would be.

Finally my attorney was brought to my cell, and of course, I was anticipating release, but I was beginning to see a pattern I didn't like emerging. Getting or buying whatever I wanted wasn't in my control at this time, and I felt more angry than helpless at my circumstances.

My attorney informed me I would be in jail, maybe one or two days.

I couldn't believe what I was hearing. He told me we should use our time wisely to create a defense for me.

A defense for me. How could I have a defense? I was there. I was angry, I pushed her. I don't honestly know if it was me who killed her or not. Didn't really care that she died, as long as it didn't affect my life. How could I have an alibi?

Oh for God's sake, get a hold of yourself, Jill, or you're damned right here and now.

Flip wanted to hear the full story and I had no choice but to tell him. I began the whole sordid tale.

"You know, Dan was a really handsome man. When he took office as sheriff, many other woman noticed this as well. Although Dan and I had been having an affair for a few years before he became sheriff, I still felt threatened by all the immediate attention he was receiving after he was elected.

Especially at that time, his wife, Emily, had so much more control over him than I did. Being young and deep in love with Daniel I just knew I wanted only him.

Malaine had always been a flirt, and had made flirtations and advances in Dan's path more than once. I just didn't really like her. I tried to overlook her as much as I could, but that day she died, she was acting kind of weird.

She'd been in the office that day flirting with Dan. Dan liked to flirt also, and he wasn't exactly ignoring her. Daniel and I ended up in a fight that afternoon over her visit. That made me furious at her, anyway.

Then much later into the evening, when Emily ran over to the sheriff's office to tell Daniel she had received a phone call from Malaine stating that since Emily allowed Dan to have an affair with me, then maybe she'd stud him out to her. Of course Malaine was drunk and rude to Emily.

That phone call pissed me off, and Dan didn't think it was so harmless, either. Daniel practically kicked Emily home and he and I walked in the dark to Malaine's house to have a talk with her. As we approached Malaine's house a large dark figure of a person was leaving and slipped into the darkness. We didn't think much about it, figuring it must have been a friend of Malaine's.

We knocked, she answered. She was pretty smashed on alcohol and mouthy. Not a good combination, alcohol and arrogance. We were really furious ourselves.

Malaine started flirting again with Dan. Dan tried to explain to her that his and my relationship was none of her concern and that her drunken public display to Emily and others made no one look good. He then told her to keep her mouth shut where he was concerned and go about her own business.

I remember the next few moments as if they'd happened yesterday. Malaine raised her voice, and said she was going to expose every dirty little affair at the law center including ours, and hers, and she could care less who it scarred. "At that remark, I reached out not even giving it a second thought, and shoved her as hard as I could, thinking you bitch, you'll not ruin anything for me. She fell with a heavy thump back into a corner. Then she looked up at Dan and I and started laughing hysterically."

We felt compelled to leave without hesitation. We did leave as quickly as possible and headed out in the dark night, hoping this was behind us. As we were walking away, I turned around to look at her house one more time and saw the large dark figure I'd seen before leaving Malaine's house, re-enter it. I told Daniel, but he said forget it and keep walking. I felt something sinister about the dark figure, but I didn't want to know.

After that night of course, the rest is common knowledge. She died, autopsy denied, she was buried. Though we were listed as suspects, nothing ever came of it, until now that is.

Flip was amazed. "Jill he said. "You have to give a complete statement and indeed tell your story. The large shadow you saw is extremely important. I'll see what I can do to get you out of here. I know you'll be a good risk for bail. By the way your bail has been set for five-hundred thousand. I'll talk to you in the morning before court. Try to get some sleep."

The next day was a cruel day in court. I was still in jail. I had to sit on the stand the entire day and tell the same story I'd told Flip over and over again.

At one point I screamed out, "Why won't you believe me? Listen to the story, this is what happened."

But the prosecution was relentless in their questioning. My testimony was too relevant to Malaine's death. They had me and wanted me no matter what I said about a shadow, or anything else.

Finally I stepped down from the stand and was escorted back to the county jail. I had another night to look forward to in jail. Dammit! Why couldn't Flip get me out? He had to get me out of jail soon, or I'd just go crazy. I didn't want to think about this mess and looking at these bars wasn't helping me.

CHAPTER 20

*T*hose few days in jail were so humiliating for me. Then I was able to make bond and was out of jail for now. However I couldn't leave town and had to stay in Preston for the remainder of the trial.

I set up house again in one of the rental houses Dan and I had owned. I guess I was fortunate my last tenant had just moved out. People I used to know, seemed supportive, but kept their distance, so as not to be associated with me. I felt like an out cast.

Court dragged on. Today they brought in Ron and Dee Roy. They were both witnesses for the prosecution. Ron had been the police radio dispatcher in charge of our law center for years, and he and his wife Dee knew and associated with everyone at the office. They were well liked by most. Unfortunately they knew a lot about the immoral goings-on at the law center as well. That included Dan and I, and the Royce family saga. They were not exactly a favorable witness for me, or my cause. All the sordid details of our sweltering love affair were continually gone over throughout the hearings.

Oh Dan, I would cry in my own privacy, why did it happen this way? Why aren't you here to cover this problem for me? But then cruel reality would hit me and I knew these events were a large part of my own dealings coming back to haunt me.

It's been over a month now, and I'm still no closer to being vindicated from this accusation, than I was when this trial began. Let's face it, I look guilty, maybe I am.

I had to give up my great job at the computer industries. I'm living in the town that has memorials for Daniel and his law-enforcement accomplishments everywhere. All my relatives are dead or gone from this area.

Is there any hope, anymore? I can't remember the last time I felt so sorry for myself. Tomorrow scares me to death. It's the last day I have to prove my case. My attorney turned out to be for himself like everybody else. There is no help.

Today would be the longest day ever. Everyone was seated and court began.

(PA): We would like to call Jill Royce Day to the witness stand.

Judge: I will remind you Ms. Day that you are still under oath.

(PA): Jill, we've been through the details of this case again and again, but let's go through them one more time for the courts sake. You had a fifteen-year affair with the sheriff of this county during that time. True?

Jill: True.

(PA): You knew Malaine Rabinski. True?

Jill: True.

(PA): You've explained to the court that on the night in question you were angry about some remarks made by Malaine, including that which she was interested in Daniel Royce romantically. Malaine was drunk when she made these comments, but these remarks nevertheless angered you into a jealous rage.

Jill: Yes.

(PA): You then stated you and your lover Daniel Royce went to see Malaine at her home the night she died. There were flippant words exchanged and in anger you, Jill, pushed Malaine down. Malaine fell

to the floor in a bent over position and because she was laughing at you, you and Daniel left in disgust. She made you angrier because she laughed at you. Is this your complete statement?
Jill: Yes, but she was alive……
(PA): No, she died. You killed her.
(DA): Objection.
Judge: Overruled.
Jill: But she was alive. (I thought to myself, this can't be happening, Dan I need you, where are you?)
Jill: There was a shadow…someone else….
(PA): You may step down Ms. Day.
Judge: Court is adjourned until tomorrow morning at 9:00a.m.

I couldn't get down from the witness stand alone. I was beside myself with worry and grief. What would I do, what choice did I have? Tomorrow my life would be decided for me.

The court was now in deliberations and tomorrow would render a decision that could forever change my life. If they find me guilty of murder, I would be sentenced to life imprisonment or face execution. I'm so confused. How could my life have gotten to this point.

With help from my attorney and others, I was in my car and on my way home. My whole life was just like a movie playing before me. I still can't believe this is happening. What to do? I know. I'll drive out to the cemetery and talk with Dan. That will calm me and Dan always knows what I need.

The drive was pleasant, almost like it could have been another time far away from this mess. As I arrived at the place where Dan's grave was, I quietly got out of the car. I didn't pay much attention to what or who might be around.

It was late evening and the cemetery was pretty empty by this time. I dropped to my knees and mournfully cried for quite a while. Pleading for relief from my sorrows, as if Dan could grant such a thing.

All of a sudden I felt a cold chill. Looking up, I was shocked to see my old rival. "Emily!" I screamed, "What are you doing here?" Emily hadn't changed a bit. She still looked like evil itself. "Jill," she said, "I've been with you all along." She went on to tell me how she had kept track of me for years. Emily said she was the dark shadow figure that Dan and I had seen lurking about Malaine's house the night of her death. That she was glad to finish the job of a jealous rage by making sure Malaine didn't get up again.

"But why Emily? Was it because of her remarks about studding Dan out?"

"No, Emily stated, "it was because of you and Dan and your sleazy hurtful affair. Malaine just got in the way and was an appropriate target for my anger at the time. I didn't mean for her to die. I had no control over the force driving me. I hate you Jill."

Then without another word, Emily put her hands around my neck. The cemetery was quiet.

The next day Jill was found strategically placed on the top of the ground where her grave was marked by Dan's headstone. The police never fully identified her killer, although it was strange she possessed the same throat marks found on the throat of Malaine Rabinski, the woman she was accused of killing.

Another chilling fact: on the other side of Daniel Royce's grave, was found the body of his estranged wife Emily. Emily was dead, a bottle of valium, her own prescription at her side. It is said she killed herself by over dose.

Did Emily plan to kill Jill, and then herself? No one will ever know, but there was a disturbing piece of evidence found. Leading away from Dan's grave, was a third set of foot prints, that led into the near by timber out of the cemetery. They were never matched to anyone.

It was all so unfinished, but the case was closed by local officials, and never spoken of without risk. Was it finally over? Who was left to tell the story? Would we ever really know the axiom of justice?

The End?

Excerpt from the second book:
Executor Takes All

written by: Ruth Forrest Glenn

It hadn't been many years since Daniel had died, when Brian had gotten a letter stating that Jill had recently died. It was a total shock out of the blue for him. The letter said that Brian needed to come to town for a meeting with Jill's attorney. It went on to say that this matter was dealing with him being the executor of her estate. Well, this is bizarre. Brian no sooner had this thought, when his phone rang. It was a man confirming flowers to be delivered to Jill's funeral. This blew him away, because Jill's funeral had been done with for a few weeks now, according to the letter. Why would this man think there was another funeral? The entire thing perplexed Brian, but he politely told the man he knew nothing about it, and that he had to go. Hanging up the phone, Brian quickly put his bags together and headed for Preston and Jill's attorney.

The four hours down to Preston was quite enough time to think matters through and ponder these things. What was this all about? Brian was interested in knowing more, but with altered caution, proceeded carefully. This trip would be submerged in thought. The thickness of the air was impassable with silence. Solitude was the key.

No one wanted to ask any more questions. Still, the eerie way Jill's death took place, and the woman she hated most, dead by her side. How could the intrigue be ignored? It had only been within weeks, since these hideous events had taken place, leaving Jill and Emily dead. Brian was the first child of Dan's to be told. Since he lived the closest in miles to Preston, and was the executor of Jill's will, he left right away to take care of any business.

The burial place of Daniel Royce was on Brian's way to Preston. He decided to stop and put flowers on his dad's grave, and pay his respects to his father. Pulling into the cemetery, he felt his heart sink. It had an insatiable atmosphere, the presence of which Brian hadn't encountered before. He stepped out of the car, and stood in the quietness of the moment. As he began to walk through the cemetery towards his father's grave, he couldn't help but remember all the times as a kid, that Dan would bring him and his siblings to the Drurry cemetery. It was always to place flowers on his parents graves, or because someone else in the family had passed away. In any case, Brian's dad would walk all the children throughout the cemetery starting from the lower southwest corner, and show them the family's lineage. No matter how many times Dan was at the family cemetery, he would always start in this particular part, and work his way up and over to the opposite side. He had a fetish about directions, and being precise with them. Brian's memory was jarred. He remembered the compass his father kept in the car. His dad was never without one. Brian had been given Dan's compass by Jill, upon Dan's death. He enjoyed carrying it with him. He reached down into his front pocket and pulled out the old tattered compass. It always brought a bitter-sweet smile across his face when he would use it. Strange he thought the needle is pointing north, but how can that be? He had never left the southwest corner, and was still standing there. Brian gave the compass a tap. The needle jumped back to the southwest direction. He thought all of this was a little weird, but it seemed alright now. The rest of the day Brian checked his compass off and on. He just hoped it wasn't broken, because it was one of the few things his dad had left him. It was irreplaceable, the sentimental value alone. Brian continued walking to the other side of the cemetery. It was the far north part he was headed for, this particular area was beautiful in greenery and the tallest willow trees he had ever seen. Just the kind of place Daniel himself thought was peaceful. It almost leaned into the eastern border of the cemetery. That was right near Dan's grave and a chunk of timber that stretched for quite a few miles. Brian couldn't imagine how many times his father must have thought about all of those cemetery visits he had made throughout his life, when he himself was dying. Brian wiped a tear from his eye, as he thought again of the last really good conversation he had had with his dad, his friend.

The old cemetery grounds were kept up well. It had a fence all the way around it, with two double gates entering and exiting the cemetery. These gates were locked each evening by nine o'clock, and reopened at six o'clock in the morning. There were a lot of head stones that were gray, with the corners crumbled. You could see the history all around you, it was a feeling that the past never left and that somehow, those who were buried there were still with us.

The beautiful green of the fresh cut grass, and the pastel colors of the many flower arrangements, collectively gave the place to bury our loved ones a sprightly mood

The Royce name was prevalent throughout Drurry, there were uncles, aunts, grandparents and such, all buried in this area dating back as far as the late six-teen hundreds.

Daniel would tell the stories, of how our great great uncle George M. Hall, had fought in the Civil War, and had been captured and placed in Andersonville, the worst Prisoner of war camp in the South during that time. After the Civil War had ended, uncle Hall was buried at Arlington National Cemetery. There was a marker at Drurry commemorating him for his service in the Union army. Dan was precariously proud of this tale. There were many things Brian's father had held invaluable. It was just a rare set of circumstances, that you were able to have him take the time to expand on them.

A loud sound disturbed Brian's thoughts. It was the ground's keeper, coming over the hill on an old tractor, lawn mower. Brian hadn't noticed him really, until that moment, and was now walking over the bluff that led to the far north corner of the grave yard where his father was buried. It was a smooth up hill walk through a grove of trees that hovered over the landscape as though to protect it in a guarding tribute. Brian had brought Daniel to the cemetery before he had died, so they could choose a plot where Dan wanted to be buried. Brian believed it was the hardest thing, that he or his father had ever had to do. It was just plain sad, he remembered.

As Brian topped the prominence, he saw his sister Ann standing at Dan's grave with flowers in her hands. Instantly Brian's own steps were suddenly at a slower pace, and not exactly because he was in control. The closer he got to Dan's grave, the heavier his feet became, and the struggle was so severe, that he set off leery of the ground below him. It was as though someone else was in authority of his feet and the movement of them. Finally he was there standing by his father's headstone. The air was chilled. A cold wave went right through Brian's body, from his head to his feet. He was still a few feet away from her. He immediately looked up and spoke to Ann, greeting her, and the feeling was instantly gone. His next thought was, how had Ann known that he was there, he hadn't called her yet. She had this phobia about ever returning to this entire area. She never wanted to visit Dan's grave alone, so what was she doing there? Did she know something no one else knew? She was glaring at the footprints. Brian hadn't even spoken to Ann, since Emily and Jill were found dead. He had tried to contact her, but was unable to catch her, and had left more than one message on her answering service. There she stood, as she looked up their eyes made a connection. Brian continued to walk toward her. "Hi Ann, how have you been? It's good to see you, but how did you find out?" Ann seemed aloof. She kept her simplistic face, and calmly said, "Oh, Kathy, yes it was Kathy. She was able to reach me at home yesterday, and I knew I had to be here." "Oh yes," Brian said, "I did talk to Kathy right after I found out our mother had died also. She didn't mention that she would call you though. She said she'd have a lot of loose ends to tie up before she could get here."

Brian thought Ann was acting unusually strange, but maybe this is how she would handle Emily's death. Never the less, Ann was there, and Kathy would be there in a couple of days, the only one missing would be Sherri, and she had just been told. Brian looked for her to arrive any time soon. Ann and Brian both stood there in the quiet.

They couldn't help but stare at the footprints that were found next to their father's grave, leading into the nearby timber. They turned to each other, blank expressions on their face. "Wonder who that was," stated Brian.

"I'm not convinced yet, but I have an idea," said Ann. Brian wasn't going to press Ann for more information right now. He knew her to be very intuitive and when she wanted others to know what she thought she would say so. Some of the footprints still had some kind of cement stuck on them where the police had tried to lift them for evidence some time ago.

"You really think you know who was here the night Jill and Emily died?" Brian said.

"Listen! Shhhhh!" Ann replied. The silence was erratic.

"Ann, there's no one here, we can talk," Brian exclaimed.

"No Brian! There is someone, and they will know."

Brian realized that Ann was serious. He wasn't sure if she'd lost her sanity for the moment, or if what she said made sense. He felt nervous and fidgeted with the compass in his pocket. It had just dawned on him to check his compass again. When he pulled it out of his pocket the needle was stuck once again, but now it pointed to the southwest corner where this whole thing had begun. This time even tapping the compass didn't move the needle back to the north where it should have been. What was the connection if any to the southwest corner and the northeast section of the cemetery. A rush of cold ran up Brian's spine. At that moment Ann agreed it was time to go. All Brian knew was that it was getting dark, and he didn't want to be locked in the Drurry cemetery until morning. Come on Ann let's get out of here. I'll follow you to the hotel. We have work to get done, to settle this thing in time for the meeting with Jill's attorney tomorrow. Maybe the others will be here by the morning.

0-595-27082-4